"I'm selling the house."

Ty kept his eyes on Camille. "George didn't want his house sold."

A flicker of guilt crossed her face. "It's my decision."

God sure did like His little surprises, didn't He? "Don't you think we should talk about this first?" Ty looked at Camille, waiting for an answer.

The only answer he got was more irritation. "What is there to talk about?"

"Funny thing, being co-owners of a ranch means we're gonna have to talk to each other once in a while."

The blank look she gave him left a cold feeling on the back of his neck. *Oh, no. Don't tell me…*

Camille's hands were back on her hips. "What did you mean by that? We're not co-owners of anything. George left the house to *me*."

Great. Ty got to be the messenger, and messengers never had it easy. "And he left *me* the land."

Christine Raymond grew up eating Chicago-style pizza, sipping pumpkin-spice lattes and plotting her way to happily-ever-afters. Following years of copywriting and one or two or three jobs that involved food, she turned to her laptop and began writing those plots instead of just thinking about them. Christine shares her amazing home with her sweetheart of a husband and oddball cat, both of whom provide their ongoing support and encouragement.

Books by Christine Raymond

Love Inspired

Finding Her Courage

Visit the Author Profile page at Harlequin.com.

Finding Her Courage

Christine Raymond

LOVE INSPIRED
INSPIRATIONAL ROMANCE

LOVE INSPIRED®
INSPIRATIONAL ROMANCE

Recycling programs for this product may not exist in your area.

ISBN-13: 978-1-335-56717-8

Finding Her Courage

Copyright © 2021 by Christine DeRenzis

This is a work of fiction. Names, characters, places and incidents are either the product of the author's imagination or are used fictitiously. Any resemblance to actual persons, living or dead, businesses, companies, events or locales is entirely coincidental.

This edition published by arrangement with Harlequin Books S.A.

For questions and comments about the quality of this book, please contact us at CustomerService@Harlequin.com.

Love Inspired
22 Adelaide St. West, 40th Floor
Toronto, Ontario M5H 4E3, Canada
www.Harlequin.com

Printed in U.S.A.

For I the Lord thy God will hold thy right hand,
saying unto thee, Fear not; I will help thee.
—*Isaiah* 41:13

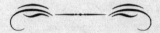

For my husband, Dan. Thank you for your unwavering support. Forever and always.

And for Co-Coe. The cat who stole my heart and made life better. Miss you much.

Chapter One

Camille Bellamy banged her open palm against the rusted window of her car, fighting to get it out of its locked upright position. The smudge-stained glass shook with a chuckle that irritated her almost as much as the twelve-hour drive turned three-day road trip when Buffy broke down in the middle of Nowhere, Iowa.

If she lost this battle too, she was going to pull her car over to the side of the road, face the great Nebraska Sandhills and let them have it until her throat went hoarse. One battle per week was all she could take.

The radio blurted something about Phoebe Saylor's celebrity wedding, then started spitting static. She banged the window again.

"Easy." Nikki looked at her from the passenger seat, locked in a battle of her own. Long blond hair had somehow tangled with the ancient seat belts. It was a toss-up on who would win. "I don't

think they have subways out here. Buffy's gonna
have to make it the whole month."

Camille drew in a breath. "Sorry. I'm just anxious to get there."

"Why don't we stop and rest?"

"When we're this close?" They were already
three days late and counting.

"George's house isn't going anywhere."

"That's probably what Dorothy said before the
tornado swooped in."

"That was Kansas. Different thing entirely."

Camille smiled, but they still weren't stopping.
It was her father-in-law's house or bust. A familiar, unwelcome thought crept in. *If Wesley...* Fill
in the blank. If Wesley were here, Buffy's window would work. If Wesley were here, they'd
have made it by now. If Wesley had never joined
the air force...

Stop. Don't do that.

Too late. Thoughts of Wesley could only be
relieved by mountains of chocolate or Evie's
coffee-colored eyes, so much like his it was almost scary. She checked Evie in the rearview
mirror. Her daughter was staring out the window.

"You okay back there, sweetie?"

Honey-colored curls bounced in her direction, and Evie's eyes met hers in the mirror. They
blinked, a thousand thoughts breathing life behind them. So much life, so much love, so much

silence. Evie shrugged and resumed looking out the window.

Camille's hands tightened around the steering wheel. Nikki slipped one hand on Camille's forearm and gave a gentle squeeze, then turned and faced the back seat, crossing her eyes and making noises like a walrus. Camille laughed. Evie didn't even crack a smile. How did a six-year-old find the strength not to giggle?

Nikki sighed. "I guess I'm not as funny as I think I am." Camille loved her younger sister for trying though.

The inside of the car was getting hot. She nudged the window's down-button again, expecting nothing. A half-inch of space appeared, and Camille's heart cried victory as the June breeze blew cool air into the stuffy car. It smelled like rain.

Something clinked. Like a spoon banging against an empty soda can. Soft at first, then louder. Camille frowned and turned her eyes to the faded yellow line on the road, searching for the source.

Nikki leaned forward in her seat. "What is that?"

A blast of gray smoke poured out from under Buffy's hood, covering the windshield and making it impossible to see anything beyond the dashboard. Camille slammed on the brakes, realized that was probably the exact wrong thing to do and eased off them so they didn't go skidding.

Nikki was breathing hard. "What happened?"

"I don't know." *Please not the radiator again.* She'd had to scrape the bottom of her piggy bank to pay for the last one, and she was all out of piggies. Patches of road peeked at her through the thick haze, and in one of them she saw a gas station up on the right.

Camille pulled to a stop beside a rusty gas pump in a four-pump station. There was a tiny garage attached to it. *What if the car explodes?* Camille thanked her inner voice for that lovely, terrifying thought and suggested Nikki and Evie get out quickly.

They slipped out and Camille urged her car away from the pump toward a small diner to the left of the station, but Buffy rejected her offer and stayed right where she was. *Goodie.* Camille wiped a strand of blond hair from her eyes, popped the hood and went to investigate.

Nikki was holding Evie away from the smoke. Camille almost managed to get the hood open without burning herself. She had no idea what to do. White smoke meant Buffy needed a rest. Black smoke meant pull over now. But gray smoke was unknown territory.

"Everything okay?" A man's deep voice rolled

toward her from the station's doors, a cross between friendly neighbor and old-style crooner.

Camille turned to look and her mind blanked. She'd never seen a real-life cowboy. Maybe once. But that was over six years ago. Most of the men in her life since then had worn military uniforms. Not quite the same thing. Dusty hair peeked out from under a Stetson hat, sending soft shadows across sun-kissed skin the color of dark sand.

"Do you work here?"

The man smiled, a crooked grin so Elvis-like she almost expected him to pull out a guitar. "No. But I know a thing or two about engines."

She noticed Nikki applying two layers of bubblegum-pink lipstick and checking her reflection in the side mirror. Wasn't twenty-six too old for boy crazy?

"Can I take a look?" Broad shoulders rolled back under a blue chambray work shirt, and Camille couldn't help the tiny flip her heart gave when he started forward.

Ty Spencer's stomach had been growling for the last hour. Ten minutes ago he'd passed hungry and stumbled into starving. If he didn't get home in the next fifteen minutes, he'd never get to eat before his one o'clock showed up. But his father had taught him better than to leave two women and a kid stranded at a gas station. Especially when one of the women had dimples the size of Texas.

Just be fast.

"We had our radiator replaced a few days ago, think that could be it?" The blonde with the dimples stared uncertainly at the engine.

"Maybe." He looked under the hood and found the problem. "It's your hose. It's busted."

"A hose?" Her right eyebrow arched, a perfect Mr. Spock.

Cute. Definitely cute. But cute meant trouble. And he was avoiding trouble these days.

"It's an easy fix." He gave her his best thousand-watt smile, generally reserved for bloggers or reporters asking about his veterans' rehab ranch. "There's no mechanic on right now, but I can make a call and get your car towed to one of the bigger places in town that are open Sundays. They should have you up and running pretty fast."

Dimples's mouth fell open. *"Towed?"* The color in her face dropped two shades, and the woman lingering off to the side hurried over. Same blond hair, same blue eyes. *Sisters.* The kid was close, but different. Her brown eyes must've come from her father.

The sister looked worried. "What's wrong?"

"We need a tow."

Even the kid looked worried now. The sister

scrunched her face. "I've got my credit card. It's not maxed out yet. I don't think." Tight money was one thing Ty could understand.

Visions of a roast beef sandwich with hot mustard evaporated. "I know the station's owner. I'm sure he'll let me in the garage. I can grab a new hose and put it in for you right here."

The look on Dimples's face was part desperation, part gratitude. "I couldn't ask you to do that."

"You're not asking, I'm offering."

But the crinkle across her brow didn't ease. "How much for the hose, do you think?"

A hose at cost was fifteen bucks, maybe twenty. He had a couple of tens tucked in his wallet he could use. "Nothing."

"Nothing?" The word started as a squeak, then rose three octaves.

Dimples's sister pinched her arm. "Don't mind her. We're from the city. My sister's naturally suspicious of anyone who smiles more than an hour a day. Offer to help someone for free and you're probably on the FBI's most-wanted list."

Dimples glared at her. "I *don't* think you're on the FBI's most-wanted list."

Ty's lips curved up. He glanced at the little girl. "Don't worry, the only list I'm on is Santa's nice list."

The kid blinked and said nothing.

"She's just shy." Dimples ran a hand through the girl's hair.

"Sure. Lots of kids are, I guess."

An old Ford pickup pulled up to the pump next to theirs. Ty tried not to bite his tongue as Liam Kendrick stepped out. He was alone today. No Mia. No trouble. Not unless Ty caused it.

For two seconds Ty thought about walking over there and telling Liam off. He knew the conversation by heart. He'd written it the day Mia left and had played it over and over in his head since then. Words like *cheater* and *liar* were peppered heavily throughout. He'd even managed to work in *pettifogger*. Ty'd had to look that one up. It meant a lawyer who uses unethical methods to get what he wants. Liam was no lawyer, but he'd certainly gotten what he wanted. Mia was his, and Ty was alone.

But the kid was watching, and Ty wasn't about to scare her just to let off some steam. He offered Liam a polite nod. Liam turned away.

Clock. Ticking.

Right. Liam wasn't the problem right now. There was a new challenge—get home before the party showed up.

"I'll get that hose for you." Ty went into the station, and when he came back out, Liam was gone. *Good.* He tossed a couple of candy bars into his truck and checked the message coming in from Dillon. Where are you?

Ty returned his brother's text. On my way. Get the plane ready.

It took fifteen minutes to get the hose changed and test it out.

He gave Dimples a warning. "It's still pretty hot under the hood. I'd grab a bite at the diner next door and let her cool down for an hour or so. They have the best banana cream pie in Sweetheart, and it's half-priced on Sundays."

The sister smiled at him. "Why don't you join us? We'll buy you a slice. As a thank-you."

It was tempting, especially when Dimples seconded the idea. "You should. We owe you that much at least."

When was the last time he'd had pie with a pretty girl? Not since Mia. And look how that had turned out. Better to avoid temptation.

Dimples pushed a strand of hair out of her face, and a wedding ring caught his eye. How had he missed that? The kid was hanging off her now, and a lightbulb flashed on. *She's married. With a kid.*

A tiny flicker of disappointment rolled over him. "Thanks, but I'm already late." The candy bars would have to do till dinner, but at least the three of them wouldn't be stuck here all day.

Dimples took her daughter's hand. "Thanks for your help."

Ty smiled. "Sure thing. Enjoy your time in Sweetheart."

Nikki held her phone toward the roof of the car, waving it around, trying to get her signal back. She looked at the screen. "Nothing."

Camille's spine stiffened. "It's around here somewhere." She slowed Buffy down as they came to a side road. A sign out front read Buggeroo Ranch.

"We passed that already," said Nikki. "Twice."

"Are you sure?"

"With a name like Buggeroo?"

Camille arched one eyebrow. "Maybe the next one." A soft breeze blew a handful of dust into her car and she pushed the up button on her window. It didn't budge.

"We should've asked that guy for directions," said Nikki. "And his name."

Camille looked at her. "What for?"

"He was cute."

"So?"

"Seriously? I have to explain cute?" Nikki shook her head and made tsking sounds.

"We're not staying in Sweetheart forever."

"Yeah, but you're allowed to date."

She shot Nikki a warning look, letting her

know she was about to cross a serious line. "I'm not here to date. We're selling the house and paying off the *b-a-n-k*."

Nikki rolled her eyes. "I'm pretty sure Evie can spell *bank*." But she must've taken the hint because she stopped talking and started waving her phone again. At least they wouldn't starve on their search. That really had been the best banana cream pie ever.

"That was it." Nikki's back went straight as her head swiveled to the right and she pointed one finger toward a stretch of road they'd just passed.

Buffy's brakes squeaked as Camille turned her head. "What? Where? I didn't see anything."

"That sign back there said Sweet Dreams Ranch."

"What sign?"

"Just turn around."

Camille did an about-face and this time caught the weathered sign with a red arrow pointing down a dirt road. She turned the corner. Tires crunched over the gravel. Everywhere around her was mixed-grass prairie stretched over what looked like miles of sand dunes.

They passed a tree with spiky branches and a thick trunk that looked older than the Earth. Wesley had pointed it out to her the one time she'd visited, right after they were married. He'd said his great-great-grandfather planted that tree.

There was a bend in the road ahead, curving up a gently sloping hill that made Buffy sputter. A house came into view, and Nikki's mouth dropped open. Evie pressed her face against the back window, and Camille leaned forward in her seat.

"That's not it," said Nikki. "It can't be. That's a mansion."

It wasn't a mansion, but it might as well have been compared to the bread box they were coming from. Five bedrooms, one for each of them plus extra. Two full bathrooms. A kitchen she could cook a Thanksgiving feast in, if she ever learned how to cook.

Nikki gave a low whistle. "The pictures didn't do this place justice. Are you sure you want to sell?"

Camille gave her sister a practiced mom look. *Don't press it.*

Nikki shrugged. "I had to ask."

George had taken such good care of the place it could have passed for new instead of rounding up its hundredth anniversary. They pulled up to a patch of greenish-sandy grass that was all the rage out here and got out just in time for Buffy's engine to let out a final wheeze. She'd be okay again in the morning, but this was her nap time.

Another ranch stood in the distance, maybe a quarter mile down the road. They had a pretty clear view of it from here even with the trees. Before he died, George had always spoken very highly of his neighbors. It was another good sign, just like the impending rain.

"Keys?" Nikki held her hands out, and Camille tossed them to her. A friendly rabbit hopped over to say hello. It wiggled its nose at them. Evie turned away and went up the porch steps.

Nothing changes, does it? Thanks, God, big help You are. At least they'd have a few weeks of fresh air.

Nikki had the keys in the door. "The first showing's at eleven tomorrow, and I can't reschedule. So just shove things into closets and spread blankets over anything dusty. I'm up for—"

Her words stopped so suddenly Camille got nervous. She hurried inside, afraid the floor had sunk in or the roof was missing. Another one of God's little jokes. But everything was fine. A little dusty, maybe, but in good shape.

"It's like something out of *Town and Country.*" Nikki moved farther into the house. "I can sell this in a week."

"Good. Maybe we can leave early."

Nikki looked at her cross-eyed. "I already took the month off. It's summer in the country. This is like a dream. Do you really want to go back to Chicago?"

"It's too quiet here."

Nikki shook her head and looked at Evie. "You like it, right?"

Evie shrugged and went to look at the kitchen.

"Why don't you get your decorator's brain working and figure out how to stage this?" Nikki was already fluffing pillows.

"I'm an *event* decorator."

"Like houses are so different? I saw pictures from that anniversary party you did. Wasn't that *in* a house?"

True. It wasn't Camille's decorating ideas that had caused her career to flop the last few months. That was stress, stress and more stress. Maybe a little decorating would ease the pressure.

The furniture here was old, but some fresh linen and pillows would make it look antiquey instead of ancient. Move the sofa away from the window and let in some light; it wouldn't take much to spruce things up.

Camille's phone started buzzing. She pulled it from her pocket as missed-call notifications flooded in. "I picked up a signal."

Nikki looked at her phone. "Really? I've still got nothing." She waved her phone over her head, then opened the front door and stepped out on the porch.

Camille's stomach did a somersault. Ten missed

calls. All the same number. She dialed Ben and his secretary answered.

"Attorney King's office."

"Hi, this is Camille Bellamy. I'm returning—"

"Oh, *Camille*. I'm glad you called. He's been going absolutely bonkers here. Hold on, I'll connect you."

A minute later her lawyer came on the line. "Camille? I tried calling you a dozen times."

"I know, I'm sorry. The reception here is nonexistent."

"Listen, we've got a prob—"

His voice cut off. "Ben…?" Silence. The signal had bleeped out of existence again. *Goodie.* There had to be a house phone around here. George always kept a landline.

A fly buzzed somewhere, irritating her already prickly nerves. She ignored it as she looked for the phone, but it got louder and louder. And closer. Camille stopped looking and stared at the open door. The sound was coming from outside.

Nikki looked around from the porch. "Is that thunder?"

"I don't think so." Evie followed Camille outside. They looked toward the gray clouds growing in the sky.

Oh, boy.

A plane's engine rumbled overhead. It was one of those personal aircrafts, the kind only rich celebrities could afford. It circled over their heads, then nosedived toward the ground like it was going to crash.

Camille let out an earsplitting shriek and grabbed hold of Evie, covering her with her body. The plane righted itself a second later, then did a full upside-down circle in the air and zigzagged between some clouds. Camille finally got it.

Tricks. The pilot was doing stunts. Over *her* house.

The pilot flew away, circled the neighboring ranch, then landed his plane on a grassy runway Camille hadn't noticed at first glance.

"Oh, no," said Nikki. "Is that an airstrip? Next *door*?" Her eyes were big. "No one's gonna want to live next to an airfield. I won't sell this place in a million years."

"Get Evie inside." Camille was already moving toward the neighbor's house.

"Where are you going?"

"To make sure that never happens again."

Ty Spencer loved flying. Nothing could change that. Not even crashing into the Pacific four years ago. Every time the wings of his plane touched the clouds, he felt a little bit closer to God. It was the thing he'd loved most about being a naval flight officer.

He let the plane's propellers come to a complete stop before turning to the redhead beside him. She still had her hands over her eyes. "You can look now."

She spread two manicured fingernails and peered through the windshield to her friends waiting at the end of the runway—four city women jumping up and down in six-inch heels that had no place on a ranch let alone the copilot seat of his Cessna 172.

The redhead looked at him with bright, hopeful eyes. She laid one hand on his forearm. "How'd I do?"

That made the thousandth time since opening Sky High Ranch he'd been asked that question. He gently pulled her hand off him and set it on the armrest. "You did great for a first-timer."

Ruby lips beamed at him as sparkly stilettos hopped out of the plane. Dillon was there to make sure she didn't fall and break an ankle. Her friends rushed her, talking over each other and stressing every couple of words.

"Oh, *wow* that was *amazing*!"

"I can't *believe* you flew so *high*!"

The redhead bounced happily in the center of them, her birthday tiara slipping sideways. "Did you *see* me? I flew with a Green *Angel*!"

"Blue Angel," Ty said, correcting her. "Retired."

"Whatever." The redhead stood, posing for pictures in front of the plane.

Dillon swatted the back of Ty's neck. "She likes you. Why don't you ask her to dinner?"

"I'm not hungry."

Since Mia left, Ty's younger brother had made it his mission to finagle love back into Ty's life. According to Dill, twenty-nine was too old for hurt feelings and bitter memories. Just because Mia had walked out on him right when Ty needed her most was no reason to avoid love forever. Time to move on. But then Dill hadn't been the one who'd buried his best friend and lost his girlfriend in less than a year.

Dillon was still talking about the redhead. He looked for someone to back up his dinner idea. "Emmitt! Hey, come here a second."

Emmitt Wilder looked over from the bench where he'd been sitting and watching the clouds. A frown etched itself across his face. Dillon called to him again, offering a wide grin and a friendly wave. Emmitt rose and walked away.

The redhead's friends were demanding their turns now, suddenly fearless of climbing thousands of feet in the air without a safety net.

Ty looked at the clouds. They probably had a half hour of flight time left unless the winds came in early. If he wanted to get the entire group up before the rain started, he and Dillon would have to split them in two. Dillon could take the second Cessna and they'd be back on the ground before the first drop fell.

"We'd better get moving." Ty started giving instructions.

A loose swag of blond hair caught his attention coming over the grassy hill. The woman it belonged to pushed past the birthday party and stopped when she saw him. Dimples creased the corners of her mouth and surprise registered on her face. *"You."*

Seeing the woman from the gas station caught Ty off guard, and he was never caught off guard. She stared at him a moment, then rolled her shoulders back.

"Are you the pilot?"

He nodded.

"What do you think you're doing?"

A nail bitten down to the quick wagged so close to him it almost bumped his nose. Soft pink lips formed a snarl that didn't fit her face.

"I'm in the middle of a lesson." Any of the waitresses at the diner could have told her where to find him, but thanking him again really wasn't necessary. "Look, don't worry about before. I was happy to help."

Dimples's mouth dropped open and eyes like the Mariana Trench spit blue fire at him. "I'm not here to *thank* you."

The birthday girl turned a peeved expression on him. "She can't cut. We were here first." Ty assured her cutting was not allowed.

Dillon motioned toward the sky. The clouds were getting thicker, and closer. Dimples was staring at him with an irate look Ty didn't totally understand. "Did you want to talk to someone about lessons? Let me get one of my guys." He looked around for Emmitt.

Hands went to her hips and sat there. "I don't want a lesson. I want you to stop flying your plane." She did a slow three-sixty, taking in the barn slash makeshift hangar where the second Cessna and the Piper Cub were holed up. "All of them."

Was she giving orders? "This is my ranch. I'm pretty sure that means I can do what I want."

A slender finger pointed toward the Sweet Dreams Ranch a half mile out. "But that's *my* house you were buzzing over. I'm pretty sure that means I get a say in things."

Her house? Ty's brow crinkled. "Are you Camille?"

Long dark lashes fluttered their surprise. "How…?"

"George talked about you all the time. I'm Ty Spencer. This is my brother, Dillon." Dillon waved hello, then started telling jokes to the birthday crowd, trying to ease their irritation. It didn't work.

A flustered look ran across Camille's face. "*You're* Ty? George mentioned you. A lot, actually. Nothing about planes though."

Ty could take a couple guesses why, but he didn't think bringing up her husband's plane crash would help the situation any. "Look, I'm sorry if the plane scared you. George never minded."

A defiant glare rolled off her face. "I wasn't scared. But I've got a showing tomorrow at eleven, and no one's gonna buy a house next to an airport."

A jackhammer started pounding on Ty's head. "A showing?"

Camille's lips pressed into each other. "I'm selling the house."

Dillon nudged him. "Ty, the rain."

Ty held up one finger, keeping his eyes on Camille. "George didn't want his house sold."

A flicker of guilt crossed her face. "It's my decision."

God sure did like His little surprises, didn't He? "Don't you think we should talk about this first?"

Dillon nudged him harder. *"Ty."*

"Yeah, just a minute." He looked at Camille, waiting for an answer.

The only answer Ty got was more irritation. "What is there to talk about?"

"Funny thing, being co-owners of a ranch means we're gonna have to talk to each other once in a while."

The blank look she gave him left a cold feeling on the back of his neck. *Oh, no. Don't tell me...*

The birthday group was standing with their arms crossed. One of them had her phone out and was typing furiously as she shot daggers his way.

Ty flashed back to the blogger from two months ago whose bad review had sent their ranch into a tailspin: Sky High Ranch = Sky High Disappointment. Another review like that and the financial dip they'd take would be irrecoverable.

He turned to Dillon. "Start up Cessna 2. We'll head up in five." Dillon hurried to the hangar.

Camille's hands were back on her hips. "What did you mean by that? We're not co-owners of anything. George left the house to *me*."

Great. Ty got to be the messenger, and messengers never had it easy. "And he left *me* the land."

The bottom of her jaw dropped toward the grass. "That's not true." Inside the hangar, the Cessna started up, drowning out their words so they had to shout everything.

"Ask your lawyer."

"I don't have to. I know you're lying."

Ty didn't like being called a liar. The only person he'd ever lied to was himself, and that was a habit he was trying to break. "Just ask him."

"No." Her dimples took an angry turn. They got bigger and deeper, more like peach pits.

"Have fun trying to sell a house without the land to go with it."

Something wet touched Ty's nose. He looked at the sky as sprinkles almost immediately turned to showers. Camille looked at him triumphantly, as if she and God had conspired against him.

The birthday group ran for their cars. Ty promised a full refund and felt the pinch in his already lean wallet. If they wanted to come back again, he'd give them each a free lesson. Anything, so long as their bad reviews didn't go viral. The redhead's irate look made no promises.

The Cessna's engine cut out and thunder cracked overhead. When Ty turned back to Camille, she was already halfway over the hill and back to Sweet Dreams.

Dillon came over. "If you hadn't argued with her for twenty minutes, we could've made it." Just the bolster Ty needed right now. "I've never seen anyone rattle you like that. Not even Mia."

Dillon had better not be playing matchmaker. "Mosquito bites are less annoying."

They watched the birthday group drive off. "Think they'll leave reviews?"

"Definitely."

"Think they'll be bad?"

"Yes." But that didn't mean their ranch had to close. Yet. "As long as we win over Phoebe Saylor and her fiancé, people won't care about bad reviews for flying lessons. Movie star weddings have a way of making people forget all that."

A smug look ran across Dillon's face. "You can thank me for my brilliant idea at any time."

Brilliant? Maybe *half*-brilliant. "Hosting a wedding is one thing. Full-service wedding planning is another."

The smug look scattered. "I had to do *some*thing. Or was it your plan to let Liam beat us out before Phoebe even got to see our ranch? He still might, you know. He's hosted weddings before. We're the newbies on the block."

Ty knew. All too well. He gritted his teeth and lightly slapped his brother's arm. "We'll be fine. Don't ruin things."

Chapter Two

Camille pulled her phone from her pocket as the rain got going. She was walking fast, but not as fast as the droplets that splashed her screen. Ben's number came up on top. *Please, God, let it go through.* But God had other plans.

Sweet Dreams Ranch was back in reach. She jumped the three porch steps and slammed the door behind her. Nikki looked up from the couch, her laptop open. Evie was in an oversize chair, staring at her feet.

"Is the Wi-Fi working?" Camille asked. She could call Ben.

"Not yet. I can't find the password. What did the neighbor say?"

Words tried forming in Camille's mouth, but all she could say was, "Phone. I need a phone." Nikki blinked, then held out her cell. "I need a phone that *works*. Where's the landline?"

Nikki shrugged as Camille's head spun. What

Ty had said couldn't be true. There was no way George would do something like that to her. But she needed to hear Ben say it.

A worried frown crossed Nikki's face. "What's wrong?"

How could she explain things without more details? "Please just help me find the phone." Nikki quit asking questions and started searching.

A small hand tugged on Camille's elbow. Evie pointed toward a side table in the corner where a black cordless phone sat beside an old-school answering machine. Camille kissed the top of her daughter's head and grabbed it.

"Ben?"

"I was hoping you'd call back. We've got a mess." Not exactly the reassurance she was looking for.

"Please say it's got nothing to do with my neighbor."

She recognized that hiss of air between Ben's teeth. Bad news. "Is your neighbor's name Ty Spencer?"

Camille was afraid to answer. "Yes. He said he owns half of George's place. But that can't be true, is it?"

Another hiss. "I'm afraid so."

Hows and whats and whys piled up in Camille's brain, overwhelming her tongue so she couldn't even get out one question. Nikki was busy mouthing words. *What? Huh?*

"Camille, are you still there?"

When had her throat gotten so dry? "I'm here."

His fancy lawyer's chair squeaked as he moved around in it. "I didn't find out about this until after you'd left. George's lawyer was late getting it to me."

"Getting what to you?"

"George's will. He amended it just before he died. Ty Spencer's name is on it. The land is his, the house is yours."

The backs of Camille's legs touched the couch. She fell into it and sat there. "Is that legal?"

She could almost see the pinched look on Ben's face. "It'll never hold up in court."

Great. So why didn't she feel better? "Are you sure?"

"Of course I'm sure. I can argue a million ways out of this. Maybe it was a typing error. Maybe the cancer got to George's brain before he died and made him unsound."

Camille's spine stiffened. "No, don't say that."

Ben paused a moment. "It might help if I did. It doesn't have to be completely true so long as it's a little true."

Camille had been with George at the end, and his mind had been the only part of him still working. She wouldn't take that away from him. "No.

If you say that about George, you won't be my lawyer anymore."

There was a second-long silence that seemed to stretched on for minutes. "Okay, I'm sorry. It was just a thought. I don't need it anyhow. Like I said, there's a million ways to argue this. Just go on with your plans to sell the place. I'll call in a few favors and have this before a judge by the end of the week. You won't even need to come back."

"You're sure?"

"Positive. Ty Spencer has a better chance of owning the Taj Mahal than he does George's land."

Camille wasn't sure that was entirely true, but it made her feel better just the same. And for now she'd take what she could get.

Nikki's voice called up the stairs at exactly 11:00 a.m. the next morning. "They're here."

Normally punctual was a good thing, but Camille had barely made a dent in the dusting. She hadn't exactly been Miss Merry Maid back in Chicago, and that was with a two-bedroom house the size of a change purse. With this place, she didn't stand a chance. She tossed her rag in the hamper and went downstairs.

"Smile," Nikki said.

Camille's mouth automatically moved up at the

corners. She'd had plenty of practice fake smiling after Wesley died. This ought to be easy.

A man and his wife who were just approaching retirement age walked up the path leading to their door. He was wearing a crisp white shirt buttoned all the way up under a navy blazer, and she wore a high-collared dress with a long skirt and pantyhose.

"Where's Evie?" Camille whispered.

"Kitchen. I gave her some paper to draw on."

Evie could spend hours drawing animals. One time she'd drawn an entire farm set right in the center of downtown Chicago. Too bad she only drew pictures. A few words here and there would've been helpful.

Camille followed Nikki onto the porch. "Mr. and Mrs. Dupont." Nikki held out her hand. Mr. Dupont gave it two hard pumps, a businessman's handshake. Mrs. Dupont touched two fingers to Nikki's, then quickly drew them back. "This is my sister, Camille." The handshakes repeated.

After a long night of tossing, turning and answering Nikki's questions as best she could, Camille had decided to take Ben at his word that he could sort this out. So she'd told Nikki to go ahead with her pitch as if everything were normal.

"I thought we'd take a look at the property first." Nikki stretched one arm out to her left.

"All of this land from the crest of that hill toward those riding trails is included."

The Duponts started asking questions. A good sign. Camille did a quick cheer in God's favor. Last night she'd actually prayed to Him. A full-on knees-on-the-floor, hands-clasped-together kind of prayer. The kind she hadn't done since Wesley's plane went down two years ago.

She'd asked Him to help her sell this place fast before the bank took her real home. He'd been pretty quiet on the subject, but when the Duponts stepped out of the house after their tour ended, Nikki flashed her a thumbs-up.

"It's charming," said Mrs. Dupont.

"Perfect," said her husband.

A steady buzz sounded over their heads, like a fly the size of a refrigerator. Camille's hands grabbed the hem of her shirt and tightened around the fabric. *Oh, no, he's not.*

The buzz grew closer, and the Duponts looked around to see where it was coming from. "What is that?" asked Mr. Dupont. "That's not your generator, is it?"

Her brain worked double-time to come up with an answer, but all she got was a big empty nothing. Ty's plane came into view and started flying circles around her house. Evie came outside and Camille grabbed her hand, wanting to shield her from the sound and sight of it.

"You live next to an airport?" Mr. Dupont didn't sound happy.

"It's not an airport." But it was hard to argue that when Ty flew his plane low enough to almost touch the roof of her house. He circled it a couple times, rolled the plane on its side, then landed back on his runway.

Mrs. Dupont gave her husband a silent look. He nodded, and Camille knew they'd lost this battle. "Thank you for your time." They started for their car.

"Wait." They looked at Camille. *Um...* "He doesn't fly his planes *all* the time."

Mr. Dupont shook his head. "Even sometimes is too much for us." A second later they were driving off.

Nikki sighed. "Is Ty gonna do that every time? He was so cute at the gas station."

When would Nikki learn? "Cute's got nothing to do with it." The problem was Ty didn't take her seriously. Well, that was his mistake. "Keep an eye on Evie." She half walked, half sprinted down the hill.

It wasn't until she passed the horse stables that she heard a squeal and realized Evie was following her. For a little girl she sure moved fast. *"Evie."* Her hands went to her hips, but only for a second. She was never really mad at her daughter, even when she was furious with her.

They'd gone too far to turn around now, especially when her blood was pumping. So she took Evie's hand and slowed her pace. They passed some horses, and prying Evie away was an unexpected challenge.

Ty was standing next to his plane when they arrived. This one was yellow and looked about five decades old. There was a boyish grin on his face, equal parts adorable and infuriating.

"What was that?" She wanted to shout but kept her voice low so as not to scare Evie.

Ty's grin widened. "It's called a barrel roll. I used to do them all the time in the Blue Angels." He winked at Evie. "Pretty cool, right?" Evie said nothing.

Blue Angels? Oh, boy, that explained things. She let go of Evie's hand and rubbed her temples. It was getting harder to stay calm. "Look, I know George liked you, but my lawyer says there's no way you're gonna get to keep the land. So you might as well stop all this."

The jokester look ran off his face. "Before George died, I promised him I wouldn't sell his land to strangers."

Nice try. "I was with George when he died. You weren't there."

She hadn't meant it as an accusation, but Ty winced. "I wanted to be, but one of our vets was… going through something. I couldn't leave him."

Vets? Like cats and dogs? All she'd seen were cows and horses. "Do you train veterinarians here or something?"

Ty cocked his head to the side. "I thought George told you about this place."

"He told me about *you*. Said you were a stand-up guy." Her opinion of Ty wasn't nearly so high.

Ahem. He did fix your car. For free.

Right. Okay, fine. She wouldn't deny he was stand-up, but that didn't mean he wasn't other things. Like irritating.

Ty motioned to the land around him. "This ranch isn't just flying lessons and cheap stunts. I've got men and women depending on this place. Flying's just how I keep it running."

Her eyes drifted toward a man with dark, twisted curls that were cut short, deep brown eyes and a prosthetic hand who was moving in the near distance. A woman with a shaved head covered in burn scars followed him with a horse.

"What sort of ranch is this exactly?"

Ty rolled his shoulders back. There was pride in his voice when he spoke again. "It's a veterans' rehab ranch. We take in military men and women who've been hurt and teach them how to be whole again."

Wow. Okay. So she wasn't expecting *that*. Still, it didn't change things. Did it? Her inner voice gave no response, so she took things into her own hands. "That doesn't mean you can just zip over my house whenever you feel like it."

"I'll do whatever it takes to stop you from selling."

Annoying wasn't a big enough word. "You're only thinking of yourself."

"I could say the same about you."

Pompous. That's the word she was looking for. Well, she wouldn't let him get to her. She turned to her daughter, seeking reassurance, and saw... nothing. No reassurance, no Evie.

Camille spun on her heels, her eyes darting left and right. "Evie?" The panic was already in her voice, her heart already mounting an unsteady rhythm.

Where was she? How could she just disappear?

Camille circled the plane and saw nothing. She ran toward the horses, thinking Evie had gotten bored and gone looking around. More nothing.

"Evie? *Evie?*" In another minute she'd be in full-on freak-out mode. Tears were already starting to rise.

A gentle but strong hand landed on her shoulder. She turned to face Ty and found the reassurance she was looking for in his eyes. "Don't worry. We'll find her."

Ty was good at dealing with panic. Two dozen men and women formed a circle around him.

Their ears twitched as Ty gave the details. Lost little girl. Six years old. He looked at Camille. "What's wrong with her?"

She gave him a look. "Nothing."

But Ty knew better. "Camille, I'm not asking to hurt you. I need to know what's going on with her if we're gonna find her. She hasn't said one word since we met. Can she talk?"

Ty much preferred Camille's Mr. Spock to the pained expression she gave him now. "No. I mean, she *can* talk, she just…won't."

"She wouldn't call out for help?"

In a low voice so only Ty could hear, she said, "She hasn't spoken for two years. Not since her father died."

He hated causing people pain, but it was better to be truthful than spare her feelings. Ty looked at the group. "All right, we're gonna have to use our eyes more than our ears on this one."

A hand attached to a tall man with a sharp jawline and cloudy gray eyes rose tentatively in the air. "Maybe she went to pet the animals. Kids like animals."

Ty almost choked on the surprise caused by the rare occurrence of Emmitt's voice. Normally when Emmitt spoke, it was in short, clipped tones. This was the most he'd said at once in the last six months.

"Good thinking, Emmitt. Why don't you take

Camille and head toward the main barn? Dillon and Daisy, can you check the hangar?"

The rest of the group split up. Ty headed for Honey, one of the few horses he trusted in extreme situations.

Camille ran after him. "I'm not staying here."

He glanced over and saw panic and guilt keeping company in her eyes. "Yes, you are."

Her voice hardened. "No, I'm not."

"You're not in the right frame of mind."

As soon as her nostrils flared and her chin tilted back, he knew he'd said the wrong thing. "Frame of mind? I'll tell you what frame of mind I'm in. I'm her *mother*."

The blue in her eyes deepened and dared him to argue, but his mom had raised him smarter than that. When a mama bear showed her teeth, you backed off.

"Do you know how to ride a horse?" A flicker of doubt crossed her face, giving her away. "It's okay, you can ride with me."

Honey whinnied casually at their approach. He stroked her deep golden muzzle and asked her to be extra good. Then he cupped his hands to help Camille up.

Deep creases formed around the edges of her lips. "You want me to get up there? Is it safe?"

He couldn't win with her. First planes, now

horses. "The others are searching on foot. We'll cover more ground if we go on horse."

Camille looked uncertain. They didn't have time for uncertainty. Ty placed one hand on either side of her waist and lifted her onto Honey's back.

A squeal, more squeak than scream, sounded from Camille's mouth. He gave her a moment to either yell at him or calm herself, and was grateful when she chose the latter. "Hang on to me," he said, climbing up in front of her.

She pinched the back of his shirt between two fingers.

"You hang on like that and you're gonna fall off." She hesitated, then pulled the back of his shirt into her palm and closed her fist over it. Ty shook his head and got Honey moving.

The second Honey went into a trot and they bounced in her saddle, Camille lost her hesitation and wrapped both arms around Ty's middle. He was surprised by the feel of something so soft pressing so close. Mia used to hold him like that. The memory was unexpected. And painful. He tried pushing it away, but that only brought out more painful memories. Jon. The crash. Mia's back as she turned away from him that final time.

"This is all my fault." Camille's voice cut through his thoughts. He half turned and saw bleary red eyes gazing back at him.

"Camille, this is my fault, not yours. I should

never have argued with you in front of your daughter."

"Do you think God will keep her safe?"

How was he supposed to answer that?

Easy. The same way he answered clients who spent their flying lesson with their eyes closed. Tell them what they want to hear. "Absolutely." It wasn't a lie. Just because God had given up on Ty, it didn't mean Evie was off His radar.

Honey's head made a sharp right and her tail came up, swatting Camille in the back of her head. She started moving faster.

"What's she doing?" Camille asked.

"Honey's part retriever. She must have heard something."

A cry so soft it was almost an exhale came from their right. Camille's head whipped in its direction. "There!"

At the base of a northern catalpa with large heart-shaped leaves and snow-white flowers was a tiny girl with a streaky red face. Evie looked up at the sound of the horse but stayed nestled where she was, holding her elbow and crying almost silently.

Ty brought Honey to a stop. Camille slid off her back, drawing Evie into her arms and holding her so tight it was a wonder the girl could breathe.

"Why did you run off? Don't ever do that again." When Camille finally let go, Evie touched her elbow. "What's wrong? Let me see." She reached for Evie's arm, but Evie pulled back each time. Fresh panic rose on Camille's face.

Ty stepped forward. "Mind if I take a look?"

Camille arched an eyebrow. There was that Spock he was beginning to know so well. "She doesn't like strangers."

"But I'm not a stranger. Not anymore."

She tilted her head, thinking, then gave a slight nod. Blond curls were matted to Evie's face. She peeked out from under them, curiosity mingling with distrust.

Ty rolled the right cuff of his shirt back and pushed it up as far as it would go, then held his forearm out to her. A long jagged scar he preferred to pretend didn't exist ran from his elbow to his wrist.

It looked like someone had tried to draw a straight line on his skin in deep red ink, and instead had decided it would be more fun to scribble outside the lines. "I got that when my plane crashed into the ocean."

Evie's eyes widened and her mouth dropped open. She reached out one hand like she wanted to touch it, then quickly pulled back. Camille was looking too, her brow all crinkled.

"It doesn't hurt," Ty said. At least not anymore. When it had first happened, he'd thought his arm had been ripped off. "I just thought it might help if you knew that sometimes grown-ups get hurt too."

Evie looked down at her own arm, bit her lip, then held it out to him. He turned it over and saw a small scrape on her elbow no bigger than a grape. No real damage a mother's kiss couldn't cure. The worry in Camille's eyes softened, though it didn't quite disappear.

"When we get back to the ranch, I'll have Emmitt take a look, just to be sure. He was an army medic."

"Is that the guy who looks like a young Clint Eastwood?"

Ty had never thought of Emmitt as Clint Eastwood, but he supposed there was a quiet ruggedness that fit the description. He radioed back to the ranch and spread the word they'd found Evie. Camille's eyes panicked again as he set Evie on Honey's back, but she held off on any objections. They were a mile from the ranch, and Evie had walked enough for today.

The gentle hum of Camille's thoughts was almost audible as they walked side by side. "Maybe I was a little harsh earlier." She paused and drew in a breath. "I'm sorry about some of the things I said to you."

"*Some* of them?"

She gave him a look. "Don't push it. You still

scared away our buyers." Her lips curved down. "But you also found Evie."

"Does that mean you'll reconsider selling the place?"

She bit her bottom lip. "Let's just talk about it later."

Ty had always preferred to fix things fast. Later would be a challenge for him, but he could handle it. He'd handled worse.

Chapter Three

Going through George's things was harder than Camille had thought it would be. She loved him, but she was irritated with him. What was he thinking giving half his property to Ty? She didn't get it. And he wasn't here to ask…or yell at or laugh with or lean on.

Enough. She was just feeling sorry for herself. It was Wesley's death all over again. For almost two months afterward, she'd refused to leave the house. Work had dried up, but her tears had refused to do the same. Evie was all that had kept her going, and then she'd stopped talking and Camille had fallen apart in whole new ways.

One day George had shown up on her doorstep. *You wouldn't come to me, so I came to you*. No accusations, no judgments. He'd just set his bag down and slept on the couch for the next month, reading silently from his Bible every night until

Camille was strong enough to resume some semblance of a normal life.

But the new normal included Evie's doctor visits and piles of medical bills. Wesley's survivor benefits didn't include outside specialists with extra long lists of initials next to their names. When George finally left, he'd slipped a fifty-dollar bill into her palm. *I can't*, she'd said.

You can.

George's letters continued bringing her fresh fifties. Sometimes there was a hundred, sometimes just a twenty. Whatever he could afford, and always when Camille needed it most.

She pulled George's clothes from the closet, feeling like a traitor. First his house, now his stuff. Would any of George be left behind once she was done?

Better his things go to someone who needs them.

There. For once her inner voice was easing the panic instead of aiding and abetting it.

His purple heart was tucked neatly on top of one of the shelves. That was staying with her. She opened the top drawer of the nightstand and set it next to George's Bible, the only other piece of him she could never part with, even if she couldn't open it.

Evie lay on the bed watching a video on her tablet. They'd finally gotten the Wi-Fi connected.

When Camille finished with the clothes, she went for the shoeboxes lining George's closet floor.

She opened the first one, expecting, well, shoes. Inside was the pocket watch Wesley had picked out for him on their honeymoon. A picture of her and Wesley together in front of the Golden Gate Bridge was in there with it.

Not now. Camille put the watch back in the box and quickly closed it, then grabbed the shoebox beside it. Inside were Wesley's Boy Scout patches and a dozen pictures of him dressed in his uniform.

The next box was more Wesley, and so was the next one. All the shoeboxes were Wesley. She couldn't give these away. Ever.

Camille's heart started beating a two-step. She stood up, taking deep breaths, and went to the window, pressing her head against the glass. Evie looked up. Her face scrunched as she got off the bed, tugging on Camille's arm.

"I'm okay, sweetie, I just got—" Scared? Worried? Felt like the world was crashing in around her? "—a little lightheaded from all the dust." But Evie didn't look convinced. She disappeared from the room, and a second later Nikki was there.

"What's up?" Nikki asked, pretending she hadn't been sent.

Camille twisted her wedding ring around her

finger. "Nothing. Going through George's stuff is harder than I thought, that's all."

Nikki bounced on the bed. "So, take a break. Go bring Ty that gift basket you made him."

Ty. There was a conundrum she didn't need right now. He was irritating, arrogant and had saved her twice in the last four days. First with the car, then with Evie. It was easier to be mad at him when he wasn't in the room.

"I'll give it to him later. I want to finish this up." And just to prove she was okay, she went back to the closet and started pulling things off the top shelf. Nikki gave her a look. The kind only a sister can get away with. "What?"

"You like him."

Camille jumped. "No, I don't."

Nikki shook her head. "I don't mean like *that*. I mean you like him. As a person. The same way George did."

There was an old record player covered in dust. Camille wiped it off and set it on the ground. "He's nice enough, I guess."

Nikki arched an eyebrow. "You baked him muffins. And you don't bake."

"It's just a thank-you."

"Well, if you don't get that basket to him soon, your *thank-you* is gonna go stale." Camille started rummaging around in a brown paper bag filled with nuts and bolts. Nikki watched her a second, then changed the subject. "I lined up another buyer."

Now that was worth talking about. "For when?"

"Couple of days."

"That long?"

"You've still got three weeks to get the bank their money. They won't foreclose early. Trust me on this. It's five years as a Realtor talking."

Camille forced a smile. "Yeah, okay."

The house phone rang. She picked up the one in George's bedroom, and Ben's voice came out in a cautious monotone. "Camille, don't freak out."

Uh-oh. Her stomach started spinning. "What happened?"

Ben let out a breath. "The judge upheld the will."

It took a second for his words to sink in. "But…how?"

"He said it was no different than splitting an estate between siblings."

Was that her head pounding, or was someone hammering next door? "Is there any point trying again?"

Ben's silence was all the answer she needed. "Camille, I'm sorry. I really am."

"Me too." She hung up with Ben and gave Nikki the news.

"Should I cancel the buyer?"

"No, don't."

"If Ty won't sell—"

"He will. I've just gotta try plan B."

Nikki drew her eyes together. "You mean telling him the truth? Because I'm in favor of that plan."

Camille stiffened. "Ty doesn't need to know about the foreclosure."

"Why not? You think he'll judge you for it? Point fingers behind your back?"

Yes and yes. She'd gotten enough dirty looks from neighbors when they'd seen the red notice taped to her door. What kind of looks would Ty give her? Camille's pride had been wounded, but it wasn't yet flattened. And she preferred to keep it that way.

"Ty is on a need-to-know basis, and he doesn't need to know."

Nikki exhaled a shrug. "Fine. So what's the plan then?"

Good question. "I'll make him an offer he can't resist."

Ty triple checked the engine on the Piper Cub. The old World War II tailwheel catered to people who found its history just as thrilling as its bright yellow curves, but its age meant there was more that could go wrong with it, and Ty didn't need the inspector coming down on him two days from now.

Dillon looked up from behind the second Cessna. "Looks okay here."

Good. Maybe they should wash them down too. The inspector wouldn't care how many bugs were stuck to the nose, but movie stars like Phoebe Saylor might.

"Did you talk to Camille yet?" Dillon's words cut into his thoughts.

"What?"

"Camille. Talk. You know, that thing people do with their mouths."

Ha. "We're still sorting things out." Camille had been avoiding him the last two days, and he was afraid to push her. Dillon came around the Piper. Ty recognized that look. "You think I should let her sell."

Dillon didn't deny it. "The money would help."

"When Phoebe Saylor books her wedding with us, we'll have all the money we need." And something even better—a reputation no blogger's post could tarnish. "Just trust me on this. Phoebe's wedding will fix everything."

Dillon folded his arms across his chest and cocked his head to one side. "You're always trying to fix things. Even the stuff you can't. Like Jon. And Mia."

Oh, good. Dillon was back on this. "I'm not talking about Jon with you."

"Or anyone else. But you need to." There was a pause. "Maybe if you had talked to someone sooner, Mia wouldn't have left."

Dillon's words cut into him—a sharp, swift punch to the gut he'd rather avoid. He fixed Dillon with a stare. *"Don't."* If his brother insisted on continuing the Mia–Jon discussion, Ty would take the Piper Cub up ten thousand feet in the air, where even Dill couldn't follow.

For half a second Dill wavered. Then he came to his senses and backed off. Kind of. "If you don't want to talk to me, there's always God. You two could use a little one-on-one time."

"God and I get along just fine." And they would keep getting along just fine if God stopped throwing out His little tests. Ditching Ty in the ocean? Test one. Killing Jon? Test two. Losing Mia? Test three. He supposed that made Camille and Evie test four.

But none of that mattered. Phoebe would be here tomorrow, and by the end of the month everything on the ranch would go back to normal. "Get the hose. We need to wash these planes down."

A light knock sounded on the hangar doors. Camille was standing with a massive gift basket in her arms. "Hi."

"Hey."

They stared at each other from across the hangar. Dillon rolled his eyes and went over to Camille. "Don't mind Ty. He forgets how to talk sometimes. I wish I could say it was oxygen deprivation from all that time as a Blue Angel, but Ty was born with his mouth taped shut."

Camille giggled. Ty glared at him. "Funny."

Dill shrugged. "I'm gonna hunt down Maricela. It's her turn to wash the planes. Camille, nice seeing you again." He left them alone in the hangar.

"Come in," said Ty. "I'll give you the tour."

Camille's eyes darted from one plane to the next. "I'm fine here." She held out the gift basket. Ty had to cross the hangar to take it from her.

"What this?"

"A thank-you."

The basket was huge. Ty needed two hands to hold it. Cookies and muffins were layered amongst multicolored confetti. "You didn't have to do this. It looks expensive."

Camille's smile curved into her cheeks. "I'm a decorator. I know how to make things look good." Right. George had mentioned that about her. "It's all homemade. Evie did the card and helped with the cookies. I made the muffins, though I guess I ought to warn you I'm not the best cook."

"I'm sure they're great. Thank you."

He set the basket on a bench, grabbed a blueberry muffin and bit in. Sawdust caked the roof of his mouth. Ty's eyes actually watered. He forced a smile, willing his throat to open up and swallow. It went down, but his stomach put up a fight upon entry.

"Delicious." Ty set the muffin aside and opened the card. Inside was a drawing of a little girl with blond curls and a man in a cowboy hat holding out an ice-cream cone to his horse.

"Tell Evie thanks for me." Camille was staring at the planes again. "You know, I used to give George lessons. No charge or anything. If you ever want one—"

"A *flying* lesson?" Her voice got squeaky. "Evie's terrified of planes. If she knew I was going up in one, she'd panic."

Ty lifted one eyebrow. "*Evie* would panic?"

"That's right."

If that was her story, Ty wasn't gonna argue with her.

She started bouncing on her feet. "Look, I said we could talk, so let's talk."

Good. Ty had worried she'd change her mind. "Okay."

She spun her wedding ring absently around her finger. "If you let me sell the ranch, I'll give you…ten percent of whatever I get for it."

Was she serious? "It's big of you to offer me part of something I already own."

"There's no guarantee you'll get to keep the land. My lawyer—"

"*My* lawyer called this morning and said a judge upheld George's will."

She pressed her lips together. "Fine. I'll give you ten percent of the sale for the house too."

"No."

"Fifteen percent."

"No."

"Twenty."

"Camille, I'm not agreeing to sell. No matter how high you go."

Her hands went to her hips. "Do you always have to be so stubborn?"

"Do you?" They stared at each other, breathing hard. "Why do you want to sell so bad anyway?"

Camille's nostrils flared and her face turned pink. "Don't change the subject. We're not done with this." But they must've been done for now, because she turned and stomped off. Ty drew in a breath, counted to three, then went back to his planes. At least they made sense.

Daisy's eyes were glowing when she ran up to Ty. "Can I meet Phoebe Saylor when she gets here? I've seen all her movies."

This was tricky. Ty wanted to say yes, but he

didn't need Phoebe thinking she'd be stalked by fans on her wedding day. "Let me see how it goes first, okay?"

Daisy tried to play it cool, but Ty could tell she was disappointed. "Sure." She had that beaten look in her eyes. The one it had taken months to turn around.

"All right, fine. Just a quick hello, then you can help Josh get the planes ready for the inspector tomorrow."

"I thought the inspector was today."

"The seventh."

"Today *is* the seventh."

Ty blinked. He pulled his phone out. *Thursday, June 7* shouted at him in bold letters from his tiny screen. *Fix this. Fast.*

"All right, new plan. Go and help Josh now, please. And grab Dillon and Maricela."

"Maricela's in town."

"Fine. Get Emmitt then." Ty thanked her and promised to bring Phoebe by the hangar during the tour. Camille's muffins were in the gift basket sitting on the entryway table. Daisy reached for one. "Careful with those."

Daisy gave him a look, then took a bite. Her face screwed up. "I…uh…oh. Who made these?"

"Camille."

She held the muffin in her hands. Her face lit up. "Maybe the goats will like them. They'll eat tin cans." She took the basket and disappeared outside.

At one o'clock, a limousine pulled up. Ty didn't think he'd ever seen anything more out of place on a ranch. Phoebe Saylor stepped out with her fiancé, an up-and-coming pitcher who might be as famous as his soon-to-be-wife in another year or two.

They were dressed in jeans and T-shirts. He'd expected Beverly Hills clothes and diamonds. Maybe Phoebe still had a little Nebraska in her after all.

Ty and Dillon greeted them. "Miss Saylor?" Ty held out his hand. She shook it warmly.

"Phoebe is fine. This is Brett, my fiancé."

Brett didn't look quite as excited to be here as Phoebe, but he shook Ty's hand just as warmly. "Please tell me you don't have rats."

Phoebe slapped his arm playfully. "You promised to be good."

Brett shrugged. "It's better to know now. Do you really want to go through all that again?"

Phoebe bit her bottom lip and looked at Ty. "You don't, do you?"

Ty had heard all about their rat situation at the banquet hall. When a hometown girl's celebrity wedding is crushed due to rats in the kitchen, it made Sweetheart's top news story three days in a row.

"No rats here," said Dillon, jumping in. "We've got a cow named Milkshake who's a real terror and keeps them away."

Brett looked confused, but Phoebe laughed. Ty led them around the property.

"This would be your first wedding here, is that right?" Phoebe asked.

Ty stiffened. "That's right." Until Dillon's big idea, it had never even occurred to Ty to host a wedding at Sky High.

Dillon cut in again. "But this definitely won't be our last. There's something charming about getting married on a ranch, don't you think?" Dillon was laying it on thick, but Phoebe didn't need convincing. She'd spent her childhood on a ranch in Sweetheart until her parents sold it and bought something smaller. They still lived in town.

They entered the hangar and Daisy let out a squeal, though she managed to keep her gawking to a minimum. Josh and the inspector didn't even look up. The inspector was pointing to Cessna 1 and jotting something on his clipboard.

Phoebe and Brett were more interested in the planes than the inspector. And they really wanted to see the barns.

"Oh, wow." Phoebe's face lit up when Ty opened the dairy barn doors. "It's like that last movie I did, the one about the cows from outer space, only this is way better. It's authentic. So much better than those CGI cows they made us use."

Brett paused beside a cow twice the size of all the others. "You know, I thought getting married on a ranch was weird when you suggested it, but now I think it could actually be fun. We can get married in a barn and take an air tour after the ceremony." He looked at Ty. "We can do that, right?"

Ty would've agreed to let them spit out the side of the plane if they wanted to. "Sure."

Brett reached for Phoebe's hand. "That's one thing this place has that Liam's doesn't. Airplanes."

Had Ty just one-upped Liam? His heart did a little dance. What would Mia think when she learned her old boyfriend had just outdone her new one? Josh appeared at the barn door. The inspector hovered behind him. Dillon excused himself.

Phoebe turned to Ty. "What about decorations? They're included, right?"

"Absolutely." Thanks to Dillon. Ty ought to put him in charge just to teach him a lesson. Instead he pointed to the rafters. "It would be easy to hang some white streamers. And we could tie white balloons to the stalls to match."

When he turned back around, Phoebe and

Brett were staring at him with deadpan expressions. "You're joking, right?" Phoebe's eyes did this thing where they simultaneously popped and narrowed. "Streamers and balloons? For a wedding?"

Uhh. He broke out his thousand-watt smile. "Of course I am."

Relieved laughter filled the barn. Brett punched his shoulder. "Good one."

The laughter died down, and Phoebe looked at him expectantly. "So seriously, what did you have in mind?"

Ty's brain did a quick breakdown of everything he knew about party decorations. Streamers? Check. Balloons? Check. What else was there?

"Actually, I don't have my ideas written out yet. Could I get them to you in a couple days?"

Phoebe and Brett exchanged a look. Phoebe frowned. "Liam Kendrick already showed us a book with sketches and pictures."

Liam had a whole *book*? That must've been Mia's idea. Just one more reason never to get involved with anyone again. Relationships didn't last, and when they ended, a mess inevitably followed.

Phoebe whispered something in Brett's ear, then turned to him. "I have to go back to LA for the weekend. I'll come by Monday, and you can show me what you have then."

Ty walked them to their limo, then hurried to find Dillon. He was talking to Josh. "There's a crack in the fuselage on Cessna 1," Josh said, skipping the preamble.

"What?" Ty thought he'd misheard. "I've checked that plane a million times."

"It's small," said Dillon. "I missed it too."

Great. "How long do we have?"

"The inspector will be back in a week or two to check again."

A week or two was plenty of time for repairs, but a crack in their fuselage was gonna wipe out the little savings they had left. That meant this wedding had to happen.

"What kind of decorations do women like at weddings?"

Dillon and Josh exchanged a shrug. "Streamers?" said Dillon.

"Balloons?" said Josh.

Ty groaned. He was asking the wrong people.

Josh nodded toward the stables. "Ask Daisy. She'll know better than us."

Good idea. Daisy was brushing down the horses when Ty found her. "How'd it go with Phoebe?"

"She wants to know what kind of decorations we'd put up for the wedding. Do you have any ideas?"

Daisy frowned. "Wedding decorations? I don't

know. I'm not exactly the wedding type." Daisy had been one of the first women trained as a combat engineer. "All I know is kid's birthday stuff. You know, streamers and balloons. Ask Maricela when she gets back from town. She'll know."

Waiting for Maricela to get back took patience Ty didn't have. Today was going from bad to worse. Dillon found him by Cessna 1 just before dinner, scrutinizing the fuselage leak.

"You okay?"

If making an even bigger mess of things was okay, then sure, he was fine.

"I had an idea." Dillon caught Ty's suspicious gaze. "Just hear me out."

Uh-oh. *Hear me out* was code for *you're not gonna like this.* Ty folded his arms. "What?"

Dillon took a breath. "Ask Camille."

Bam, there it was. The best worst idea ever. "No."

"But she's an event designer, right? George said she was great at it."

"No."

"Why not?"

Did Dill really have to ask? "She won't do it. Not unless I let her sell the house." Dillon pressed his lips together. Ty fought back a groan. "You and I have been through this. I promised George."

"Yeah, but you made a lot of other promises too. Like to the people on this ranch."

Ty glared at his brother. "You really know how to dig the knife in, don't you?"

Dillon shook his head. "I'm not trying to. I'm just saying that George was a vet too. He put the needs of military men and women above his own, always. If there was one reason to break your promise to him, saving this ranch is it. And it's one he'd understand."

Why did Dillon have to start making sense all of a sudden? Money from the sale would only cover expenses for a few months, but Phoebe's wedding would restore their reputation. More flying lessons, more riding lessons, more events. The money would continue coming in even after Phoebe was gone. He had to make sure she chose him over Liam. Still...

"I don't need Camille's help."

"If we get Phoebe's wedding, we'll have less than a month to plan things out. A professional event decorator would be a pretty big help. Don't you think?"

Yes, but Ty had always managed to figure things out on his own. This was no different. "I haven't even talked to Maricela. She'll know what to do."

"She just got back."

Ty wiped his hands on his jeans. "Where is she?"

Inside the kitchen Maricela was setting bags

of groceries on the table. Emmitt was helping her. A pink bandanna with a unicorn covered her burn scars today. Some days she didn't need the bandanna at all, but self-consciousness was a tricky thing.

"Hey, I heard about the inspector," she said. "Sorry."

But that was a headache for tomorrow. "Do you know what kind of decorations women like at weddings?"

Maricela stopped what she was doing. "The Saylor wedding? Did you get it?"

"Not yet. We're close, but she wants decoration ideas."

Maricela's eyes lit up. "Oh, sure, that's easy."

Ty felt the tension leave his shoulders. He grabbed a pen and pad off the counter. "Ready."

"Okay, well, white balloons, maybe with something sparkly tied to the ends. And streamers are always good." Ty's heart sank. "Oh, and those little candy-coated almonds. I had those at a wedding once, they were really good."

Ty looked at Emmitt. "What do you think?"

Emmitt shrugged. "What Maricela said."

Ty put the pad and paper down and went outside. The lights were on at the Sweet Dreams Ranch. Ty took two deep breaths, counted to three and started over.

Chapter Four

The porch swing was squeaking, and it was driving Camille batty. She found a rusty oil can in George's garage, but she must've been oiling the wrong spot, because the squeak was still there.

Nikki poked her head out the front door. "Are you still at it? You're obsessed."

"I'm not obsessed. No one's gonna want a house that squeaks."

"I don't hear anything."

Camille's mouth dropped open. "You don't... *Listen*." She pushed the swing. The squeak made her ears hurt.

Nikki shook her head. "Don't be weird in front of the buyers. I've got two coming tomorrow. And one of them is a retired pilot, so planes aren't an issue. Is that okay?"

Okay? It was great. "Yeah. Why wouldn't it be?"

Nikki tapped her foot and set her hands on

her hips, a move she'd learned watching Camille. "Ty."

Ugh. "Don't remind me. Just keep doing what you're doing. I'll figure out the rest."

"How?"

"I just will." She went back to her oil can, and Nikki went back into the house.

Oil spilled on the wood, leaving a stain. Camille grabbed a rag and tried wiping it up, but she only spread it out and made things worse.

"Cat litter." Ty's voice made her jump. Her foot knocked over the entire can and slick golden goo puddled on the porch. She sat the can back up, but the damage was done.

"Sorry. I didn't mean to scare you."

Camille glared at him. "You didn't. What do you want?"

He pointed to the stains. "Kitty litter will soak up the oil, just like on a driveway. I've got some if you want it."

She wasn't giving in to his Mr. Nice Guy routine. "No, thank you."

"If you change your mind—"

"I won't." How hard did she have to grit her teeth together to make him go away? "Did you want something?"

The sun dipped in the sky, silhouetting Ty with pinks and purples that almost made him look like he was blushing. She looked closer. He *was* blushing. "I need your help with something."

A favor? From her? No way. But curiosity wasn't easily dismissed. "Help with what?"

"Do you know who Phoebe Saylor is?"

"The movie star? She's from here, right?" Phoebe Saylor had been all over the news lately. That whole thing with the rats was just gross.

"Right. Well, turns out Phoebe's got a thing for ranch weddings."

Camille arched an eyebrow. "Not *your* ranch?"

"Maybe. It's between me and another rancher right now, Liam Kendrick." Ty's face lost the blush and grew tight. If his teeth were gritting any harder, they'd start breaking. "She came by Sky High today and loved almost everything about it."

Whatever Ty was getting at must have been hard for him. He wasn't the type of man to fumble, and he was fumbling all over the place right now.

He drew in a breath and spit out his words. "She hated my decoration ideas and I have no idea what to do. George always said you were this amazing decorator and I thought maybe... you could help."

If there was a punch line, she didn't get it. "You're not serious?"

He came up the porch steps and lowered his

voice, a whispered conversation between cowboy and city girl that caught Camille off guard. "Our ranch isn't doing great. Financially. One of our planes needs some repair work that's gonna wipe us out. If we get this wedding, it fixes everything."

She felt bad for him, but she didn't see what it had to do with her. "I'm sorry, Ty, but I can't help you." If he thought she was gonna play friendly neighbor now, he was kidding himself. She grabbed her oil can and headed inside.

Ty's voice came dangerously close to panic. "You can sell the house."

Camille paused with her hand on the door. She turned back around. "What did you say?"

"You can sell the house, but only if you help me. And only if Phoebe Saylor picks Sky High for her wedding."

Hmm. "What would I have to do exactly?"

He tossed his hands in the air. "Dillon told her decorations were included, and she's expecting something better than streamers and balloons."

Camille paused. "You didn't actually suggest that to her, did you?" Ty's blush was back. It was almost endearing. *Almost.* "So, if I give you some ideas, you'll let me sell?"

He shook his head. "No, you've got to meet with her. Actually plan things out and see them through to the wedding day. After she's married, you can sell the place and we'll split the profits according to George's will."

Camille frowned. "When's the date?"

"The last Saturday in June."

"That's in three weeks." Good for her, but bad for planning a wedding.

"They already sent out invitations. Phoebe's brother got time off from active duty. It's way too late to change things."

Tempting. "We have two buyers coming to look at the house tomorrow. You promise not to scare them off?"

"Promise."

On the inside Camille was already halfway through her happy dance. "When do we start?"

"Phoebe's out of town this weekend. She gets back Monday and expects something spectacular, otherwise I'm finished."

Tomorrow was Friday. That was plenty of time to come up with spectacular. "I'll be at your place tomorrow at nine."

Ty was in the barn with Emmitt when Camille and Evie showed up the next morning. He kneeled down so that he was eye level with Evie, then held his hand out. "Good to see you. Ready to dig your hands in and get them all greasy?"

Evie scrunched her face up.

"She's shy," Camille said. But a second later

Evie's hand shot out and grabbed hold of Ty's. She pumped it with a wrestler's strength, and Ty pretended to fall over like she was crushing his fingers.

Evie didn't giggle exactly, or smile, but there was a light in her eyes that told Ty she hadn't forgotten how it was done. Camille looked shocked Evie had even moved.

Milkshake mooed, vying for their attention, and Evie went to say hello. Worry lines dug across Camille's forehead. "Is it safe for Evie to pet her? What if she bites?"

Ty stifled a laugh. "Cows can't bite. They don't have upper teeth. The most they can do is gum you, and Milkshake won't even do that." Evie climbed onto the bottom rung of Milkshake's gate and was busy stroking the tips of her ears. Milkshake was busy loving it. Camille still looked uncertain.

Emmitt popped up. He'd been laying down some hay in Milkshake's stall. "Milkshake's friendly. She's only in here alone because she had a cold and we wanted to separate her. I'll keep an on eye on Evie for you."

The worry lines eased. "Thanks, Emmitt." Camille looked around the barn, taking it in from floor to ceiling and wall to wall, then dug out a notebook and pencil. "Do you know if they want to be married inside or outside?"

"Inside, I think. Or maybe outside. I don't know, I guess. I could text her." Why hadn't he thought to ask when she was here?

"That's okay. I'll come up with ideas for both." She walked toward the ladder that led to the loft, scanning things with a professional eye and jotting down ideas.

Ty peeked over her shoulder. "*Clotheslines?* I don't think Phoebe Saylor's gonna want clotheslines draped across the barn at her wedding."

Camille's head snapped around. "They're for pictures. We string clotheslines around the barn and hang pictures of the bride and groom off them, mixed in with the lights. It's rustic. And charming."

"I don't think Phoebe wants rustic."

"She's getting married on a ranch. She'll be fine with rustic."

Good point. "All right, sorry. Go ahead."

Camille's eyes drew together, but she went back to her notebook. She circled the barn, peeking into the stalls. He moved a little closer, getting behind her again. He just wanted to see what she was scribbling.

A quick sketch of the barn from one end to the other was spread horizontally across the paper. Camille had penciled in all the posts, beams and doors. Around the posts she'd drawn some sort of swirly something and an arrow pointing away from them saying *white lights*.

Ty shook his head. "No white lights."

Camille jumped and almost bopped him in the nose with her head. "Are you gonna sneak up on me like that all day?"

"No. It's just that Phoebe's not into stuff like that. When I suggested white balloons and streamers, she hated the idea."

"That's because they were balloons and streamers, Ty. Not because they were white." She shook her head.

Ty backed off. "Sorry, just trying to help."

"If you want to help, then stand back for two minutes and let me get my thoughts down. This is just the barn. I've still got to look at the stables, the property itself…the hangar." Her last words came out shaky.

Ty took three steps back as Emmitt and Evie came over. "I think Evie wants to see the horses." Emmitt held out a piece of paper Evie had taken from her pocket and given him, and Ty saw a pretty good drawing of a horse. "Is it okay if I take her to the stables?"

Camille started fidgeting. He'd only known her a few days but already he knew the routine. It started with a foot shuffle, followed by a few twists of her wedding ring. "You won't let her ride one, will you?"

Emmitt's eyes widened. "Oh, no, nothing like that. She can help brush them though. And we've got some oats she can feed them."

The fidgeting settled down. Camille let go of her ring. "That sounds nice. Thanks." He and Evie walked off, and Camille started drawing in that notebook of hers again. The one Ty wasn't supposed look at. The one that held his future in its pages.

Ty stood where he was for as long as he could, but his feet were itching to move. He grabbed some hay and added it to Milkshake's stall, then picked up a shovel and hung it on the wall, glancing at Camille's notebook as he went past. "Mason jars? I think Phoebe's expecting more than mason jars."

When Camille spun around, the look in her eyes was enough to rattle the toughest cowboy. She threw her notebook on the ground. "Okay, that's it. If you want decoration ideas, ask Milkshake." She started for the barn doors.

Just couldn't keep quiet, could you? Ty chased after her. "Camille, wait. I'm sorry. Please don't go."

She twisted around, ready to combust. "Why not? You can still criticize me when I'm not here."

Criticize? Is that what he'd been doing? Camille just got under his skin in a way most people didn't. Not even Mia. Danger signals started flashing at the comparison, and Ty snapped them off before they went any further.

"You're right. I'm sorry. I didn't mean to criticize you. I'm just out of my element here, and I'm not used to that."

Camille's glare softened. "This is never gonna work if you're constantly second-guessing me."

"I know. I won't."

But *DOUBT* flashed across her face in neon letters. Ty had to make this right. Truth time. "I've got two dozen men and women counting on me to fix a mess that I created. If I don't get this wedding, the ranch might have to close."

Camille's brow crinkled. "You created? What do you mean?"

This wasn't a story Ty liked telling, but if it meant the difference between her staying or walking out those barn doors, there was only one option.

"A few months ago, this blogger and her friends booked a flying lesson. They showed up drunk. I refused to take them up and refunded their money. The blogger wrote up some pretty nasty stuff, and our sales took a nosedive." He sighed. "I guess her blog was more popular than I'd realized."

A frown spread across Camille's face. "It doesn't sound like you did anything wrong."

Ty shrugged. "Tell that to social media."

Camille stood where she was a minute, then slowly crossed the barn, picked her notebook off the ground and dusted it off. Ty hadn't realized how much tension he was holding until he felt it seep out of him. "Thank you. I promise to stay out of your way."

A soft smile played on her lips. "You'd better, or I might have to get your brother to tape your mouth shut."

Dimples the size of Texas sprang up in the corners of her cheeks. She turned back to the hay-lofts, and Ty's heart gave the tiniest of patters. Those dimples were dangerous.

Camille's feet crunched as they stepped onto the front porch Saturday morning. She looked down at the light gray granules sprinkled across the wooden flooring, covering yesterday's oil stain. Nikki paused behind her in the doorway. "What is that?"

There was no point fighting the smile rising on Camille's lips. "Kitty litter." Ty must have brought it over late last night, or early this morning. "It's to soak up the oil." Nikki shrugged and started down the path.

A small hand wove its way into Camille's and squeezed. It took Camille by surprise. Usually she had to initiate that sort of thing with Evie. Maybe next she'd get a smile. And after that an actual word. Camille hadn't given up on her daughter yet, despite what the doctors said.

Nikki bounced along. "I still can't believe Ty agreed to let you sell. I guess he's as sweet as he is cute. Think he's seeing anyone?"

Camille's head snapped around. "What?"

Blond hair fell to the side. Nikki's eyes drew together. "Don't worry. I was only kidding."

"I'm not worried." But Camille heard the crack in her voice.

Nikki was still staring at her. She moved in closer and whispered so that Evie couldn't hear. "You don't like him, do you? I mean, roman—"

Camille stopped her right there. "No, of course not." But Nikki didn't look convinced.

Whatever. Nikki could push all she wanted, but Camille wouldn't be interested in a superhero, let alone a pilot. Even if Ty was nicer than she'd first thought. Once he'd relaxed yesterday, they'd actually had fun. But that sort of kindness had to be an act. There was definitely something wrong with him. There had to be.

The barn doors were open when they showed up. She was half expecting Ty to still be asleep, but he was talking to Dillon. A box of equipment sat on the floor between them.

He turned when they came in, and Evie actually went over and gave him a hug. She never did that with people she'd just met. For a split second Camille was too startled to talk. Then she regrouped. "Thanks for the kitty litter."

Ty grinned. "No problem."

She introduced Dillon to Nikki, and her sister's bubblegum-pink lip gloss appeared. Three coats this time. Camille tried not to roll her eyes.

"What's this?" she asked Ty, tapping the box with her foot.

"Just some notebooks, measuring tape, that sort of thing."

That was nice of him. Maybe a little too nice. "So, you're just leaving me with this while you go watch TV?" No wonder he was awake. He wanted to push this stuff off on her and get out of here fast. There was probably a ball game on.

Ty looked confused. "What? No. I'm yours for the day. I only thought this might help."

Oh. Nikki gave her a look, and she felt the pink rush to her cheeks. "Sorry. Sure, this is great. Thanks." She started sifting through the box and pulled out the measuring tape. "Is it okay if Nikki walks around and takes some pictures?"

"Sure."

Dillon jumped forward. "I can show you around if you want."

Apparently the lip gloss had worked. "That'd be nice," said Nikki. Two minutes later they were gone.

Ty gave Evie some hay so she could feed Milkshake. She ran to the stall with it. "Emmitt and Maricela offered to take Evie around when they feed the rest of the animals, if that's okay."

Aha. "You don't want Evie hanging around? Not much of a kid person, I guess."

Ty blinked. "I just thought she'd like to see the animals. She almost cracked a smile yesterday. Maybe today we can actually pull one out of her." He paused a second. "And I love kids."

Camille started twisting her wedding band around. "Sorry. Guess I'm just a little tired today."

It was easy to read Ty's expression. Crossed eyes, head tilted to the side, slight frown. *What's with you?* But there was nothing with her. She was just a little jittery. Too much coffee, probably.

Emmitt and Maricela came by and took Evie to feed some goats. She made Emmitt promise the goats wouldn't eat Evie's fingers, then played if off like she was joking when they all laughed. Silently she told herself she'd do a finger check as soon as Evie returned.

"Did you want to check out the hangar?" Ty asked when she was done in the barn.

Camille's heart bumped against her chest a little too hard. "Is that another barn I saw on the other side of the storage shed?"

"Yeah, we've got a few. This is just the main one."

Perfect. "I think we ought to focus on the barns for now. And the stables. I was thinking Phoebe might like to be married at the stables, then ride a horse to the barn for the reception." She arched one eyebrow, waiting for Ty to shoot down her idea.

"That's a great idea."

"It is?"

"Yeah. I'm sure she'll love it." His mouth curved up at one end. Very Elvis. Very cute. She forced the thought away. "Your client list in Chicago probably comes with a one-year wait list."

If only. "Why is that?"

"Because you're really good at this. Smart and pretty is kind of a rare combo."

Camille bit her bottom lip. The word *charming* crept into the back of her mind and lingered there. The warmth in Ty's eyes did nothing to push it away. She brushed a strand of hair from her eyes and saw him glance at her ring. She put her hand down to her side and headed for the next barn.

A couple hours later she was all barned out and ready for the stables. They were bigger than she'd realized. She could string lights across the top and add a bouquet to the door of every stall. She sketched out a few ideas, expecting Ty to peek over her shoulder, but he stayed three feet back. Definitely on his best behavior today.

"There's a lot of outdoor space here," she said. "We ought to think about how to use it. Where's a good place to set up chairs?"

Ty looked around. "There's a shady spot back toward the house that's pretty nice. Lots of trees." He started walking, and Camille followed. Nikki's tour must have ended, because she and Evie were leaning over a fence, throwing chicken feed on the ground.

A rumbling sound started up from the direction of the hangar, and a white plane with a blue stripe on the side pulled out. Camille's heart gave an uncomfortable lurch, and her feet got tangled up with themselves. She fell forward.

Ty's hands shot out and grabbed hold of her, wrapping around her waist and pulling her back up. They stood that way for a minute, then Ty cleared his throat and stepped back as the plane sped down the runway. "You okay?"

She nodded. Her mouth was too dry to talk. The plane lifted off the ground, and Camille looked quickly away. Ty gave her a reassuring smile. "Dillon's giving a lesson, but don't worry, I told him not to buzz your house."

Camille would have thanked him if her heart wasn't speed-walking down a runway of its own. "Do you have to fly planes? Couldn't you just give riding lessons or something?"

"We tried, but the money wasn't enough to keep this place going. Flying turned it all around."

That was all well and good, until one of the planes crashed. Evie was staring toward the sky. "Maybe we should call it a day. Evie doesn't like planes. She'd probably be more comfortable at home."

There was that look on Ty's face again. Half-irritated, half-adorable. "She looks okay to me."

"She's not." Camille started toward her.

"Hang on." Ty hurried to catch up.

"Don't worry, we'll be back tomorrow."

Ty touched her shoulder, and she paused just long enough to meet his eyes. "We go to church Sunday mornings and usually hang around for a bit afterward, chatting and helping out with things. We won't be back till noon. Maybe even a little after."

"That's fine. Evie can sleep in."

"You're welcome to join us. I mean, I don't know if you ever go to church, but it's a pretty nice one if you do."

They used to go to church all the time, but that was before God had taken Wesley from her. "Thanks for the offer, but I think we'll pass for now."

Ty nodded. "Sure, the offer's always open though."

Not just charming. *Likable.* "We'll see you tomorrow around noon then." Camille turned away from him fast, before something more dangerous than *charming* and *likable* got into her head.

Chapter Five

Camille hadn't realized how much she wanted Phoebe to like her ideas until it was her last day to come up with them. Back in Chicago Camille's boss had branched out from birthdays and anniversaries to weddings. Camille had only done a handful, but they'd gone well and she'd hoped to do more. Then the banks had started calling and the bills had started piling up. If Ty's finances had taken a nosedive, hers had been swallowed up by a black hole. And her focus had been swallowed right up with it.

If she went back to Chicago with Phoebe Saylor's wedding in her portfolio, it would help undo some of the damage the last few months had done. Her boss might even start sending her on jobs again instead of confining her to a desk, and the yearlong wait list Ty mentioned the other day might actually become a reality.

She got Evie out of bed, dished up a late breakfast and was at Ty's by eleven thirty. Evie veered them toward the hangar; Camille veered them toward the barn. Her notebook came out, and her pencil started moving fast. Evie tugged on her arm, and the line Camille was drawing swerved right. "Sweetie." It was more tsk than reprimand.

Evie pointed toward the stall where Milkshake had been just yesterday. It was empty. Worry lines that belonged on a thirty-year-old etched themselves across Evie's forehead.

"I'm sure Milkshake's okay. When Ty gets back, we'll ask him." But Evie's worry lines only added another five years. When Ty finally showed up, it was almost one, and Evie was two steps from forming a search party. She knocked the breath out of him with a hug, then grabbed his hand and tugged him toward the stall.

Ty picked up on the problem pretty fast. "Milkshake's fine. Remember we said she had a cold? Well, she's better now, so we moved her back in with the other cows. She missed her friends." Evie stopped tugging Ty and started dragging him toward the barn doors.

"Evie." Camille put her hands on her hips, a sign that things had progressed past the tsk-phase. Evie immediately let Ty go.

"Why don't I get Emmitt?" said Ty. "I'm sure he wouldn't mind paying Milkshake a visit." Evie turned wide eyes to Camille, who nodded her okay. Her notebook was still clutched in her hand, the blank page desperate for her attention.

Ty returned with Emmitt a few minutes later. "I heard you want to see Milkshake?" Evie nodded. "Funny, she said she wants to see you too."

One corner of Evie's mouth flickered, like she meant to smile. But then she sneezed and the flicker dipped back down. The light in her eyes stayed right where it was though. She gave Emmitt a hug, then took his hand and led him out of the barn like she knew where she was going.

Two hugs in less than thirty minutes? That had to be a new record. Maybe Nebraska agreed with Evie more than she'd thought.

"So how was church?" Camille's notebook was open again, her pencil sketching about ten miles too slow. Why couldn't her hands keep up with her brain?

Ty kicked some hay. "Fine."

Her pencil paused mid-stroke. That didn't sound like the same Ty who'd talked the church up to her just yesterday. She arched an eyebrow. "Fine?"

He shrugged. "You know, church is church."

Hmm. Maybe she wasn't the only one conflicted about God. *Okay, new subject.* "I hope it's okay we came by early. I was anxious to get started." If they actually got the job, it meant

Camille would have roughly eighteen days to plan a wedding fit for a movie star. If she had her boss's entire Chicago staff working for her day and night maybe, *maybe*, she could get it done. Trapped in Nebraska, without all that, she had no idea how to pull it off.

That crooked grin Camille loved so much curved across Ty's face. Much better than the frown that had started forming. "Sure. You and Evie are welcome here anytime."

Kind, cute, genuine. She officially gave up trying to find something wrong with him and accepted the fact that Ty was just a nice guy.

Did you say cute?

Camille told her inner voice to pipe down. So what if Ty was cute? So was Evie. So was Milkshake. There were a lot of cute things in the world. Ty just happened to be one of them. An hour later, her sketchbook was half full but her brain was still bursting with ideas. "Let's check out the other barns."

"Again? What about the hangar?"

A slick, icy wind ran up her spine and over her neck. "No, um…the storage shed."

Ty's brow crinkled. "What would Phoebe want with the storage shed?"

She gave him a look. "You said you wouldn't second-guess me."

His hands flew up and zipped his mouth shut. "Sorry. Force of habit."

They headed over, but Ty was right. The storage shed really wasn't right for a wedding, even a rustic one, no matter how Camille tried to spin it. She spent a good hour in there anyway, but couldn't make it stretch any longer. That only left one place she hadn't explored.

"Ready for the hangar?" Ty asked.

Dark clouds only Camille could see circled the hangar, a thunderstorm about to strike. "I need another look at the stables."

Ty gave her a look but kept his opinions to himself. They started down a short path. The stables were unchanged since yesterday, but Camille didn't let that stop her from spending an inordinate amount of time going through them. New ideas. New sketches. Anything to keep her busy and away from the hangar.

Ty's phone buzzed. He slipped it out of his pocket. "It's Phoebe. I texted her last night to ask about an indoor or outdoor ceremony."

"And?"

"And she and her fiancé want to get married in the hangar, then fly out in one of the planes."

Fly. Out. In a plane. Camille's head couldn't quite wrap itself around that.

"She'll be here tomorrow at ten. Is that good for you?"

Her voice croaked. "Sure." She cleared her throat. "I'll be here at nine. We can go over things one more time before she gets here."

Ty stopped walking and folded his arms across his chest. "So. Do you want to see the hangar now?"

There was no way out of it. "I guess."

Three planes gleamed brightly at her as Ty opened the hangar doors. The space was huge. Other than the planes, there wasn't much in here, except the smell. Grease and oil and all things bad. You could actually feel it get inside you and rot there. She'd smelled it a thousand times when she'd visited Wesley on air-force bases.

At least there was plenty of room to dance. She jotted down a note to ask Phoebe whether she was going with a band or a DJ. Ty went over to the yellow plane and patted it affectionately, like a kitten. Camille didn't get it. How could you feel affection for something that could kill you?

"I think I've seen enough." She turned and exited the hangar without waiting for him.

Ty jogged after her. "You really hate planes, don't you?"

Hate? No, she didn't hate them. Exactly. She just hated how dangerous they were. "They have their place in the world, I guess. Like most things. It's Evie who hates them."

There was that look again. Like he was choosing his next words carefully. "Can I ask you something about her?"

Camille's defenses went up fast. It was habit when it came to Evie. "What?"

"Has she really not talked in two years?"

That was an easy one. She'd only answered it a billion times before. "Yes. Not since her dad died."

"What about doctors?"

She shrugged. "What about them? We went to every doctor in Chicago and a few that weren't. They all said the same thing—give her time."

That was every doctor's first, last and final prescription, always accompanied by a handful of pills to turn her daughter into a mindless zombie. A midsize fortune had been spent on what amounted to false hopes and a big pile of nothing *but* time.

"I remember when George found out about Wesley. I'd never seen him so sad." Ty paused. "I'm sorry I never got to meet him. He sounded like a great guy."

Even two years later it was still weird hearing people talk about Wesley in the past tense. "Thank you." Her voice came out thick and her eyes drifted toward her shoes. There was a very interesting piece of dirt stuck to them.

"I know it's hard. My friend Jon was a pilot too. There was a storm and his plane…" Ty didn't have to finish. The same past tense that had stuck in her throat got caught in his.

"I'm sorry."

"Thanks."

But that only made Camille's head hurt harder. How could Ty keep flying after something like that? She'd never understand him. Spending the entire day with him had only confused her further. "I think we've got enough ideas here to wow Phoebe tomorrow. I know she's picking you over Liam."

A new shadow passed over Ty's face. Dark. Forbidding. Camille was no fool. Whatever was between him and Liam went deeper than Phoebe Saylor. But then the shadow vanished and his smile returned.

Evie came running toward them. Her face was pink. If she'd also been smiling or laughing, she'd have looked like a totally normal kid.

"Time to go, sweetie." But Evie wrapped her arms around Camille's waist and shook her head. "It's almost dinnertime." When had five o'clock rolled around? But Evie's head kept shaking, stronger and more frantic. She sneezed once, but that didn't slow her down.

Emmitt was hovering behind them. "I told her she could brush Honey later, and she hasn't gotten her chance yet." He looked sorry.

"If you want, you can eat dinner here, with us," said Ty.

The effect was instantaneous. Evie's eyes started glowing. Was it eating with Ty, or the idea of brushing a horse? "I guess we could." All she'd had planned was spaghetti. "Is it okay if Nikki joins us?"

"Sure." Ty's trademark grin appeared. "You're always welcome here, remember?"

Ty set out three extra places at the table. Camille took the seat beside him, and Evie squeezed in next to her. Dillon waited until Nikki was seated before making his decision. He shooed Maricela away from her usual spot and slid in on Nikki's other side.

Tonight was Ty's turn to say grace. Camille looked a little flustered but bowed her head and instructed Evie to do the same. Evie looked confused but did as she was told.

There was plenty of food to go around. Anything they didn't eat got packed into the fridge for lunch the next day. Fried chicken, roast beef, potatoes… It took a lot of food to feed two dozen mouths.

"What does Evie like?" Ty asked. "Fried chicken?" He'd never known a kid who didn't like fried chicken.

"She loves it." Camille thanked him and handed him Evie's plate.

"How about you?" His hand was already

poised over a wing. Something told him Camille could eat her weight in wings.

"Actually, I'm a vegetarian." Two dozen men and women dropped their forks on their plates. Camille's face turned pink.

"Really?" Ty wasn't upset, just surprised. Vegetarians weren't common in Nebraska, especially on a ranch. He put the chicken down and scratched his head. "I'm not sure there's anything here—"

"It's okay. There are plenty of side dishes to fill me up." She reached for the mashed potatoes.

Maricela stopped her. "I'm sorry. I used chicken broth when I made them." She looked guilty, like Camille might think she'd done it on purpose just to mess with her. "I didn't know."

Camille's smile outweighed Maricela's frown. He got the idea she was used to stuff like this. "Don't worry about it." Next to the potatoes were the brussels sprouts. She grabbed those instead.

Dillon cleared his throat. "Uh… I wouldn't. Pork fat."

Camille looked down at the bowl in her hand and made an involuntary face that did nothing to diminish her dimples. She set the bowl down.

"I can fix you something in the kitchen," Ty said.

But Camille shook her head. "No, it's okay. There's already so much food here. I'll be fine." Her eyes moved up and down the table.

Everyone was watching her. Ty gave them each a look, sending silent signals to stop staring and start eating. One by one, they picked up their forks.

Camille reached for the macaroni and cheese. "Ham," Daisy said, almost jumping in her seat.

He'd never realized how much meat was at their table. Maybe he ought to make everyone get their cholesterol checked. "Let me make you something."

Camille's smile grew a little forced. "No, no. I'm good with salad."

She already had the salad bowl in her hands when Josh stopped her. "I'm sorry. Bacon." She put the bowl down. The dimples were gone. "Well, the bread looks good. Is it homemade?" She reached for a slice.

Enough was enough. Ty pushed his chair back. Camille looked at him, her mouth already opening in protest. Ty took her hand and pulled her up. He hadn't expected the touch of her fingers to make his heart dance. It started as a waltz, but slid quickly into a disco.

Stop this. Now. Do you want another Mia?

But that was ridiculous. Ty wasn't infatuated with Camille. He was just… They were neighbors. Simple, easy and uncomplicated. For the most part.

"Come on. I'm not gonna let you starve." He

pulled her gently toward the kitchen and was relieved when she followed.

There were stools all around the breakfast bar. Ty pushed one out for her. "Do you eat eggs?"

"Yes."

"How about an omelet?"

Her frown eased ever so slightly. "That sounds good, but you really don't—"

Ty cut her off with a look. "I don't let guests go hungry. Especially guests who've been busy helping me all weekend."

There. It was just the edge of her dimples, but he was pleased to see them starting back up. He reminded himself that dimples equaled danger, but it had little effect. You could admire the *Mona Lisa* without hanging it in your home. Not that Camille was the *Mona Lisa*. She was just a girl. Smart, funny…beautiful.

Don't. Ty cleared his mind.

Camille's eyes brightened. "All right, you can cook, but I've got one condition." Ty braced himself. "You've got to let me help."

That was one condition Ty could live with. He opened the fridge. "What do you like? Green pepper? Onions?"

"Yes and yes."

He handed her some veggies and grabbed two chopping knives. Ty cut into the onion, but he forgot to run it under water and his eyes started tearing up. Her dimples widened.

"You think it's funny seeing me cry?" He fake sniffled for her.

"It lets me picture you as a little boy. I bet you threw better tantrums than Dillon."

"What makes you say that?"

"It's in the eyes. His are mischievous, but in an obvious way. Yours are more subtle. The kind of kid whose tantrum sneaks up on their parents. That's always worse."

Ty grinned. "And here I thought I was being all mysterious. Turns out you had me pegged from the get-go."

"That's life experience talking. One kid plus a half-finished business degree and you're basically an amateur psychologist." She giggled.

"Business degree?"

Camille hesitated. "I wanted to start my own event company one day."

"Why didn't you finish?"

There was the tiniest pause before she answered. "Wesley got deployed mid-semester. We got married before he left, and I found out I was pregnant while he was gone. Going to school *and* working *and* being a mom was a little much."

Too bad. She seemed like an amazing decorator. The kind who deserved her own company. He threw butter in a frying pan and turned the heat up. "I'd figure you for a three-egg omelet, but then I thought you were a wing girl."

"Three eggs is good." He cracked three in a bowl and she got up from the stool to join him at the stove.

"How long have you been a vegetarian?"

"Ten years. I saw the kind of documentary you shouldn't watch if you enjoy eating meat. I just couldn't look at it the same again."

"But before that, you were a wing girl, right?"

She was standing so close they bumped shoulders. "Absolutely." She picked up the bowl of eggs and dropped them in the pan. Melted butter splattered and she jumped back, cradling her hand.

"Are you okay?" Ty took her hand without even thinking about it, wanting to see how bad the burn was. He held it gently in his as a red welt began puffing up.

"I've got a first-aid kit under the sink." He grabbed the ointment and reached for her hand again.

"That's okay, I'm fine."

"You need to treat it or it'll blister."

She reluctantly gave her hand back. The burn was mostly on her palm, but a little butter had splashed onto her ring finger and left its mark there too. He moved the ointment around, trying to avoid her ring but accidentally brushing against it. Camille's hand jerked back.

"I'm fine now, thank you."

"Just let me get you a bandage." He was already reaching into the first-aid kit.

"I said I'm fine." Her whole body was stiff.

"Camille—"

"I'm *fine*, Ty. What do you not understand about that?" She was spinning her wedding ring around. Ty tried not to be irritated by it. There was no reason for him to be. They were neighbors. *Just* neighbors.

Keep telling yourself that.

Ty's back grew rigid. "You're just being stubborn."

Camille's glare intensified. "No, I've just been taking care of myself for a long time and don't need you doing it for me. I'm not helpless."

"I didn't say you were."

"Then stop treating me like a child."

"I'm not. You've just got a stubborn streak the size of Texas."

"Well, your control-freaky nature is stampeding all over my stubborn streak."

The chatter on the other side of the kitchen door died down. Camille and Ty glared at each other.

"Maybe I'd better go. It's close to Evie's bedtime."

"It's only six o'clock."

Camille paused. "She goes to bed early." She moved for the door, and Ty flashed back to his last fight with Mia. Same door. Different woman walking out of it.

Except Camille's not Mia.

And Liam wasn't stealing her away. Ty was pushing her away all on his own.

"Camille, wait. I'm sorry. I didn't mean to upset you."

"I'm not upset." She pushed the door open.

Ty followed her into the dining room. "Camille, come on."

She kept her back to him as she got Evie out of her seat, then hurried out of the house with an almost inaudible, "Goodbye." Nikki sat there a minute looking confused, then gave Ty and Dillon an apologetic smile and hurried after them.

Ty stood there dumbfounded. How had things gone so wrong so fast?

Dillon looked over at him. "Don't worry, Camille's not the first person your cooking's driven away. I'm sure she won't be the last."

Maricela threw a dinner roll at him. "You are so not funny."

Chapter Six

The sun had only been out a few minutes when Ty went into the kitchen and started coffee. He needed a minute alone before the day began and two dozen veterans came down the stairs depending on him. Phoebe would be here in a few hours. This last weekend with Camille would either fix everything or be all for nothing.

Nothing?

Okay, maybe not nothing. Ty liked spending time with Camille. Maybe a little too much. No more of that. Even if Ty wanted to move beyond the friendly neighbor phase, which he didn't, he'd be fighting an uphill battle. It was hard enough competing against a flesh and blood man; what chance did he have against a memory?

From now on, no more dinners, no more joking around, no more fun. Things with Camille were business, pure and simple. His emotions would stay in check, and the situation under control. Just how Ty liked it.

He took his mug into the living room and flipped the light switch. Something moved in the easy chair and he almost jumped.

"Emmitt? What are you doing?" Other than sitting in the dark. Alone.

He does look like Clint Eastwood, doesn't he? Tall and strong and brooding.

Emmitt didn't say anything right away, and Ty's eyes shifted to the mug in his hand. Emmitt caught the look and obviously knew where Ty's mind was going. "It's coffee." He set it on the side table.

Ty nodded and tried to push his doubts off, but not staring at that mug was like trying not to breathe. "Want some breakfast?"

Emmitt stood up. The mug stayed where it was. "Maybe later." He walked out of the room, and Ty scooped the mug up. Empty. He held it to his nose. It smelled like coffee.

Dillon came into the room. "Thought I heard voices. Talking to yourself again?"

Ty's glare was enough to silence Dillon's jokes. "Emmitt was in here. Alone. In the dark."

Dillon understood where Ty was going. "Oh, no."

"He said it was just coffee, but I don't know. Who sits in the dark drinking coffee?"

"Emmitt." Dillon crossed the room and took the mug. He sniffed. "Smells like coffee to me."

"Yeah, but what if—"

"Benefit of the doubt. Remember? We promised him."

Easier said than done, but he would give it a try. His own coffee was getting cold. Dillon followed him into the kitchen and poured himself a cup, scooping mountains of sugar into it before dousing the whole thing in cream. "What time is Camille getting here?"

Ty hesitated. "Nine, I guess."

Dillon looked up. "You guess?"

"Well, that was the plan before she stormed out of here last night."

"What was up with that anyway?"

But it was too early in the morning to talk baggage, especially when it wasn't his. "She thought I was treating her like a child."

"Were you?" Dillon sipped his coffee.

"No, I was just trying to help her."

"You mean like how you're *always* trying to help *everyone*?" He stirred his spoon around his cup. "You know what Jon would say?"

Ty wasn't gonna do this. "I do. A lot better than you. He'd tell me to get my head together and concentrate on Phoebe. That's what's important right now."

"Ty—"

But he was done. He rinsed the rest of his coffee down the sink and left the kitchen.

When a car pulled up at eight o'clock, Ty was sure it was Phoebe. *She's early.* Panic set in. Camille wasn't here yet. He quickly dusted his hands on his pants and closed the gate to the stables.

The car door opened, and Ty's panic evaporated as a dog the size of a football came running out. Hot chocolate, liquid smoke and whipped cream mixed together to create the color of Co-Coe's fur. She danced around his ankles with a voice more whisper than bark as he bent over to pat her head.

"Been a while since I've seen you." The dog licked his hand, and Avery waved to him from her car. He waved back, kicking himself for not recognizing it sooner. He called out to her. "How've you been?"

Avery pulled dark brown hair into a low ponytail. "Busy. Is Emmitt around?"

Good question. "He was inside last I saw him. Does he know you're coming?"

"I told him. Whether or not he heard me is up for debate."

Now Ty understood Emmitt's moodiness this morning. Avery started for the house. Ty called after her. "Hey, don't let Emmitt squirm his way out of your talk. If he runs, go after him."

"What do you think I brought Co-Coe for? Best attack dog ever." She called for Co-Coe, who wagged her tail and gave Ty a final lick, then shot to Avery's side.

Ty went back to his work, and when he checked the time again it was nine fifteen. His neck went stiff. Camille still wasn't here. There were no voice mails. No texts. Maybe the time on his phone was wrong.

He went into the house and checked the clock hanging over the fireplace. Nine seventeen. Imaginary waves crashed over him. For one second he was back in the Pacific Ocean and Jon was calling out for help as lightning struck over their heads and thunder cracked around them.

Ty focused on the clock, trying to push the thought away, but the clock wasn't doing it for him. It was Camille who popped into his head. Not Mia or the laugh that used to drive him wild. Not a flash of the soft caresses he'd missed so much since she'd walked out the door.

Camille.

Her eyes were bluer than the Pacific could ever hope to be. They smiled, and Jon's cries faded away. Ty took a deep breath. It had been a year since he'd had that kind of panic attack.

Get it together. You're fine. You've got it all under control.

Right. Ty had this. He just needed to figure out

where Camille was. She'd said nine o'clock, and now it was… Ty's heart stopped. Nine twenty-five. How long had he been standing here? He dug his phone out and dialed Camille's number. No answer. He sent her a text and stared at the screen. Still no answer.

Was she really gonna stand him up because of a silly fight? After all the work they'd put in?

Avery's voice came down the hall. "Emmitt, stop. Let's talk about this."

Emmitt entered the room and froze when he saw Ty. Gray eyes bounced from him to the front door. Avery was walking so fast she almost ran into him. "Emmitt, come on. You can't keep running from me."

For a second it looked like he might respond. Emmitt's mouth opened and his lips parted, but then they closed again just as fast. Emmitt made a beeline for the door and got out of there before Avery could stop him.

Her shoulders slumped. "Have you ever met anyone more stubborn than my brother?" She wiped her eyes and forced a smile. Co-Coe zipped out of nowhere and started whisper-barking around her ankles until Avery picked her up.

The dog licked her face, and Avery's smile grew a little less forced. "What are you up to?" Maybe she wanted the distraction. Or maybe she could tell Ty was having a moment of his own.

He could use a sounding board right now either way. "Phoebe Saylor's gonna be here in—" he looked at the clock again "—twenty-five minutes. And the woman who's been helping me is missing."

Avery stroked Co-Coe's fur. "You mean Camille?" She arched her eyebrow. It wasn't the Spock look Camille got away with, but it wasn't bad.

"Have you met her?"

"I saw Dillon in town the other day. He filled me in." She set Co-Coe down and the tiny dog went to investigate a piece of lint. "How late is she?"

Ty didn't want to think about it. "She was supposed to be here at nine."

Avery winced. "You tried calling?"

"Yeah."

"And texting?"

"Repeatedly."

Avery shrugged. "Well, I'm no decorator, but I know enough not to suggest balloons and streamers. If you want, I can stick around till she shows up."

"You don't have to do that."

"I don't mind. At least then my visit wouldn't be for nothing."

Ty wasn't sure that was such a good idea. This was Camille's gig, and he'd already stepped on her toes enough times to make them bruise. He checked his phone again. No voice mails. No texts. Twenty minutes left. If Camille was leaving him in the lurch, it meant she was leaving him with only one choice.

Camille dropped Nikki and Evie off at the house, then stepped on the gas. There was no time to walk. She couldn't believe how late she was. Buffy sputtered white smoke as she came to a stop outside the barn. She hopped out, assuming Ty was already inside.

The doors were open, and she ran in. "Hi, sorry I'm—"

Ty was standing next to a slender woman with long dark hair and gray eyes. They were shoulder to shoulder. Camille's "sorry" wavered on her tongue. A practiced smile forced itself onto her face.

She couldn't tell if Ty was happy to see her or if she'd interrupted something. He walked toward her. The woman followed. "Where were you? I thought you weren't coming."

Camille blinked. "Why would you think that?"

Ty's crooner voice lost the croon and sounded more like an out-of-tune piano. "You're forty-five minutes late. I called you a dozen times. I thought you were still mad about yesterday, so I asked Avery to help out."

Avery. Was that her name? Camille's eyes moved to the left. Avery was smiling at her. Camille would not be won over that easily.

"I'm no decorator or anything," said Avery. "Everything I know comes from those home makeover shows."

Uh-huh. Stay calm. Deep breaths. She turned back to Ty, wanting to yell, but her jaw felt wired shut. How could he bring in someone else to help him? This was her project; she had notebooks full of ideas. Didn't he like them? Didn't he trust her? Her teeth started grinding. "I texted you."

Ty's brow bunched up. He pulled his phone out, pushed some buttons and held the screen up for her to see. "I didn't get it."

Nice try. Camille looked at her phone. All three texts she'd sent Ty were there, along with little red flags just beneath them. Could not be sent. Oh. She swallowed her embarrassment and forced another smile. "I forgot my phone loses its signal every two minutes out here. I'm sorry."

Avery put her hand on Ty's shoulder. "See? I told you she'd be here."

It took Avery a full thirty seconds to take her hand off Ty's shoulder. Not that Camille was counting. "I had to go into town. Evie woke up sick."

At the mention of Evie, Ty's irritation softened. "Sick? Is she okay?"

"She's fine. Just a cold. Nikki's with her." Nikki had said it was only a cold, but Camille wasn't taking chances. She'd thought a doctor's visit would take twenty minutes tops, but that was before she'd realized Sweetheart had never heard of urgent care.

"Well, I guess I'm not needed anymore," said Avery.

Ty looked at her. "I'm sorry, I totally forgot. Camille, this is Avery. Avery, Camille." They shook hands. Avery's were small and sweaty. "Camille, Avery is Em—"

Daisy ran into the barn. "Heads-up, Phoebe's limo just pulled in." She saw Avery and broke into a grin. "I thought I saw Co-Coe running around out here. Come say hi to everyone." She gave Avery a hug and they both offered Ty and Camille a thumbs-up as they left the barn together.

Phoebe walked in. She was alone. "Do you know there's a car smoking outside your barn?"

"Smoking?" Ty took a step toward the doors.

"It's just Buffy," Camille said. "She'll be fine in a few minutes."

He grinned at her. "You named your car Buffy?"

But Camille wasn't gonna let Ty off the hook just because he smiled at her. He'd brought in outside help. That was even worse than thinking she wouldn't show in the first place. But now was not the time to get into it.

Camille started walking Phoebe through her ideas for the barn. She loved them all, especially the clotheslines with the pictures.

"Of course, we can set it up the same way in the hangar, if you want the reception in there instead. Ty mentioned you wanted to…fly out after you're married." It was hard to think about, and even harder to say out loud.

"Actually, I don't know about that anymore. I like what you were saying about the stables. Getting married on horseback would be like something out of a fairy tale."

Ty shot her a thumbs-up, but Camille held fast to her irritation. They wrapped things up back at the barn.

Phoebe's face was glowing. "I don't want to say anything for sure before I talk to Brett, but let me just say that I *loved* your ideas, Camille." She looked at Ty. "I'll call you by tomorrow and let you know either way."

The limousine driver came around and opened Phoebe's car door for her. She got in and they watched her drive away. Ty tapped Buffy's hood. The smoke had stopped. "You know, if we sell George's place, you can probably buy a new car."

New car? Buffy wasn't going anywhere. And anyway, she had way more important things to take care of than cars. "Any money I get is going to the bank so they don't take our house in Chicago." The words were out of her mouth before she realized she'd said them.

Ty's face tightened. "I'm sorry. I didn't realize things were that bad for you. Why didn't you say something? I'd have never have put up such a fight about selling."

And there was the pity. Lurking just behind it would come the judgment. Exactly what Camille didn't want or need.

"It's none of your business. I'm sorry I said anything." She knew she was being testy, but meeting Avery had pushed all the wrong buttons.

He tried changing the subject. "How about we celebrate? We can pick up Evie and get lunch out somewhere."

"Evie's sick. She's not going anywhere."

The crooked grin he was giving her turned upside down. "Right, I forgot." He rolled back on his heels. "Look, Camille, I'm really sorry about last night. If I said or did anything…"

Did he really think she was still upset about last night? "I've gotta get back to Evie. Let me know if you hear anything." She started Buffy up and white smoke puffed out. Just one puff, then it went away, and Camille went home.

Camille closed the front door harder than she meant to. Nikki looked up from the couch, elbow deep in a bag of chips and a can of bean dip.

"So?" Nikki sat up.

"Phoebe loved my ideas. She'll let us know by tomorrow." Nikki jumped up for a high five. Camille tapped her hand with two fingers and went into the kitchen.

Nikki followed. "Everything else okay?"

"Fine." She took some orange juice from the fridge and poured a glass. "How's Evie?"

"Asleep. No fever, just the sniffles."

Good. Camille downed the orange juice, but it wasn't enough to get rid of the sour taste in her mouth. Nikki leaned against the wall. "All right, what happened?"

Camille set the glass on the counter. "Nothing."

She went upstairs to check on Evie, and when she came back down, Nikki was standing on the bottom step, blocking her path. "It's obvious something's bothering you. Just tell me."

Fine. It would probably be better to get it off her chest anyway. "Ty didn't get my texts. So, he asked some other woman to meet Phoebe with him."

Nikki uncrossed her arms. "What woman?"

"I don't know. Avery something. They were talking decorating ideas when I got there." She went back into the kitchen.

"Did Ty have another decorator on speed dial

or something?" Nikki didn't sound nearly upset enough.

"No, I mean, she wasn't really a decorator. She was just helping out till I got there."

The little crinkle that had formed on Nikki's face flattened out. "Oh, so what's the problem then?"

This was no time for jokes. "Are you serious? He was talking to another woman. Decorator, I mean."

"But you said she wasn't a decorator."

Why was Camille letting Nikki fluster her like this? "She's not, but…but that doesn't mean she won't swoop in and try taking credit for my work."

Nikki frowned. "You know, you sound a little jealous right now."

Jealous? Of what? Nikki was getting this all wrong. "Why would I be jealous?"

Nikki hesitated. "Are you sure this is all about decorating tips? Maybe you like Ty a little more than you want to admit."

Camille's feet started shuffling. They stared at each other. "I like him fine. As a neighbor." So long as he didn't buzz her house again, she'd continue liking him just fine.

"Are you sure that's it?"

"If you're trying to help, you're doing it wrong."

But her sister was the master of not letting

things go. "You know, Wesley would want you to be happy."

"I am happy." She moved out of the kitchen and into the living room. Nikki followed her. Camille went upstairs to her room. Nikki kept on her heels. "I want to take a nap."

"In a minute. I just want to say one thing, then I'll stop. I promise."

It was better than listening to her for the next hour. "Make it fast."

Nikki drew in a breath. She kept her voice low so as not to disturb Evie. "You're allowed to have fun and enjoy someone's company. Liking someone isn't the same as loving them."

Camille put her hand on the door. "Is that it?"

Nikki bit her bottom lip. "If you did like Ty, and I'm only saying *if*…" Her eyes drifted to Camille's hand. "Then wearing your wedding ring all the time might send him the wrong signal."

An unseen hand crushed Camille's heart. If that was Nikki's best advice, she could keep it. "I'll be down later." She shut the door and made it to the edge of the bed before her knees began to give, and she sat down before she fell down.

Why did thoughts of Wesley have to hurt so much? She looked at her ring and twisted it around her finger. There was no way this was coming off. There was no reason to take it off anyway. Nikki was way off base with everything she'd said.

She lay down, and Wesley's face flashed in front of her, but it was followed by another less familiar face.

George's Wi-Fi was pretty good here. She grabbed her phone off the side table and did a quick internet search. There were thousands of videos of Blue Angels zipping across the sky in their planes. She clicked the first one that came up, then lay back and watched a plane circle through the air and move into a barrel roll, wondering if it was Ty she was watching.

Chapter Seven

Ty couldn't stop grinning. He grabbed the kitty litter and a broom and tossed them in the back of his truck, then headed over to Camille's. It was way too early to knock, but Ty couldn't sit still. Not after Phoebe's text. The kitty litter he'd laid down last time had gotten knocked around by the wind. He swept it up and tossed it in a trash bag.

The stains were better but still visible. He laid down fresh litter then stepped on it to make sure it settled in. One of the floorboards was loose. Ty put his full weight on it to test it out, then bent down for a closer look. A nail had popped out. An easy fix. He dug his tools out of his truck and started hammering on the floorboard.

The front door squeaked open and Camille poked her head out. "Ty?"

"Sorry, I should've left the hammering till

later. I didn't mean to wake you." He stood and faced her.

"You didn't." Her eyes moved to the floor. "What are you doing?"

"Your floorboard was loose, so I'm fixing it."

Tiny dimples creased the corners of her mouth. She stepped out on the porch and closed the door behind her. "It's seven in the morning."

That was late on a ranch, but he'd known she kept to city hours. "I was up."

"Is that more kitty litter?" The dimples cranked up another notch.

"I figured if we're gonna sell this place, it should be at its best."

A V-shaped crinkle formed right between Camille's eyes. "Well, we're not ready to sell just yet. We haven't heard back from Phoebe."

He didn't know how he kept his face straight. "Actually, we have."

The crinkle deepened. "We have?"

He nodded and unleashed his grin. "We got it."

Camille's dimples cranked all the way up and she pulled Ty into a hug. It felt good to hug her instead of bicker with her the way they'd been doing.

Her voice was soft when she spoke, a light dusting of powder against his skin. "I'm sorry for flying off the handle yesterday." Rosy cheeks were a good look on her, but Ty didn't need her embarrassment or her apologies.

"Don't worry about it. I haven't exactly been at my best temper either. It was kind of a stressful weekend." He hesitated. "Kind of fun though too." *Careful. Business only, remember?*

But Ty loved seeing that sparkle in her eyes. Her hands flew up and almost hit his nose. "Oh. Today's the twelfth. That means the wedding is in two and a half *weeks*. We've gotta get started. I have a thousand things to do."

"I already thought of that." Ty pointed to his truck. "I thought we could pick up whatever will fit and set up deliveries for the rest. Then get some ice cream."

She blinked. "Ice cream?"

"To celebrate. Banana Blitz opens at nine. The hardware store is already open, and the craft store will be open by the time we get to town. How's Evie?"

"Better. Her throat isn't as sore, and she slept through the night. She'll probably be fine in another day or two."

"Think she'd like it if we brought her back a sundae?"

"I think she'd love it. Give me five minutes." She went in the house and Ty put his tools away.

When she came out again, Nikki was with her.

"I've got more buyers coming this week, so don't go buzzing your planes around."

"I won't."

Nikki grinned. "And tell Dillon not to go buzzing anything either, or I'll have to pinch him."

"If I tell Dill there's a surefire way to get pinched by you, he'll be flying circles around this place all afternoon."

Nikki's grin widened. She promised to call Camille if anything happened with Evie, then they headed into town.

Camille filled up a cart at the hardware store, and Ty put it on his business card. He hardly ever went into craft stores, and Camille had fun taunting him with yarn.

"I'll have to teach you to knit so you can help with the decorations."

He paused beside some bright yellow yarn. "What are we knitting?" He'd never so much as picked up a ball of yarn before.

"We need a thousand chair socks by tomorrow. But don't worry, it's easy."

Did she say... "Chair socks?"

"Yep." She stared at him with a totally deadpan expression. Ty stared back, then broke into a grin.

"You actually had me for a minute. *Chair socks.*" He picked the yellow yarn off the shelf and threw it at her as she ducked and burst into giggles.

"For the record, chair socks are a real thing." She put the yarn back on the shelf. "But I wouldn't use them at a wedding, and I have no idea how to knit."

Next up, ice cream. Dorie, the owner, greeted them inside the shop. Ty told Camille to pick out anything she wanted. Just one condition.

"What's that?"

"It's gotta be at least two scoops. Maybe even three."

She grinned and he paid for three two-scoop hot fudge sundaes, including one to bring back for Evie, which they'd pick up when they left. Outside on the picnic tables, just two bites in, Camille got fudge on her nose. Ty laughed, and when she demanded to know what was so funny, he handed her a napkin. She wiped her face, embarrassed but adorable.

Stop. This. Now. Business only.

But ice cream *was* business, wasn't it? They'd been working all morning, so that made this a business meal. Pure and simple.

A woman's voice sounded behind them. "I should've known I'd find you here, stuffing your face." Ty turned. Co-Coe sat at Avery's feet wagging her tail. She whisper-barked at Ty, then ran over and tried to jump in his lap. Ty picked the dog up and stroked her soft fur.

When he looked at Camille, her spoon was

sticking straight up out of her sundae and her hands were clenching the tabletop. Maybe it was Co-Coe. Some people were weird about dogs getting too close to their food. He put her down and she ran to the other side of the table, resting her paws on Camille's legs, looking for the same treatment.

Camille gave the dog a friendly pat but kept her other hand white-knuckled to the table. Avery rested one knee on the bench beside Ty. "So, what are you guys up to?"

"Phoebe called. We got the job."

Avery squealed and gave Ty a hug. "That's amazing." She beamed at Camille. "I knew God sent you to Sweetheart for a reason."

Camille's face turned three shades of red, but she didn't look embarrassed. More like angry. If Ty had only just met her, he might not have been able to tell the difference, but working side by side with her this weekend was enough to clue him in.

Dorie opened the door and poked her head out of the shop. "I saw you two out the window. Guess what I've got?" She kneeled down and held out a Puppy Paws ice-cream cup. Co-Coe sprinted for it. Avery chased after her. "Nice seeing you again," Avery called over her shoulder.

Ty returned to his sundae. Camille stirred her spoon around, not eating.

"Are you okay?"

She blinked. "What? Oh, yeah, I'm fine." A forced smile ran across her face and she started eating again. But she kept her eyes on Avery as she and Co-Coe headed away from the shop.

Invisible fingers snapped in place. Ty finally got it. Camille was still upset about Avery helping out the other day. This was his fault. What could he say to make things right? "I've known Avery awhile now. I think you'd really like her if you got to know her."

Camille pushed the rest of her sundae to the side. "I'm sure I would. Do you see a lot of each other?"

"Mostly just at church."

Camille's head tilted to the side. "Church?"

"Yeah. She's there most Sundays."

A thin crease formed in the corners of Camille's eyes. "You know, I was thinking about your offer the other day, to go to church with you. And now that you mention it again, I think Evie and I would like to take you up on it."

"That would be great." Maybe if she saw Avery at church, she'd be able to put the other day behind her. A month from now they could be best friends.

Camille won't be here a month from now.

His stomach churned at the reminder, and two scoops didn't seem like such a great idea anymore. But it didn't matter where Camille was a month from now. This was just business. That wouldn't change a week from now or a month from now. Or ever.

It was already Thursday, and Camille felt like it was just getting started. In Chicago it had taken Camille months to put together a wedding. Here she had sixteen days.

There was a team of people helping her in the barn. Maricela and Josh were cleaning out stalls, Dillon and Nikki were stringing lights, and now that her cold was gone, Evie was helping sort through the hundreds of pictures Phoebe had emailed over yesterday.

Camille had almost had a panic attack when she'd learned Ty didn't have a photo printer, then he'd taken her to a copy center in town, and she'd gotten them done in half an hour.

"Is this right?" Nikki called down from the ladder.

Camille looked over and saw she'd wrapped the lights up the post horizontally. "It looks great, but I think they'll be better at a diagonal. Maybe you can scooch them around without unwrapping the whole thing."

"Will do, boss." Nikki gave her a little salute. It was the third time today she'd done that. What Nikki didn't know was that if she kept it up, she was gonna be calling Camille "boss" at home from now on too. She guessed it wouldn't stay funny for long.

Camille walked over to check on Evie. She had successfully sorted two hundred photos by size and was now starting on the final hundred. "Good job." She kissed the top of Evie's head.

Evie looked up, not bored exactly, more like antsy. She'd been sitting in the same spot since this morning. She reached into her pocket and handed Camille a folded-up drawing of Milkshake and Honey. Both had big smiles on their faces. If only Evie would smile like that.

"You can visit with Milkshake and Honey in a little bit, okay? I promise."

Emmitt entered the barn with an empty wheelbarrow. Camille was relieved to be getting the dirty hay out of here. It was one thing to have hay at a wedding. It was another thing entirely to have hay that animals had been sleeping in, sitting on and who knew what else with. He'd made a dozen trips with the wheelbarrow already and still wasn't done. "Thanks, Emmitt."

He smiled shyly at her. "I don't mind helping."

Okay. Dirty hay out, clean hay in. Her plan was working. Except for Ty. He was still busy with the plane-repair guy, and it was taking forever. She'd give him ten more minutes, then hunt him down.

Next up on her mental checklist were Josh and

Maricela. They were sweeping out the stalls. "How's it going?" They were all smiles, but the push broom kept slipping out of Josh's prosthetic hand.

Camille watched him drop it, pick it up, then drop it again. If he hadn't insisted on broom duty, Camille would never have given it to him. She was on the verge of asking him to do something else when Maricela pulled her aside.

"Don't worry about Josh. This is good for him. He wants to figure out how to do this stuff for himself. That's why we're here."

Camille nodded. "Understood." When he finally got the broom to behave as he wanted, a satisfied smile spread across his face.

Ty really was doing a lot of good with his ranch. She was happy Phoebe had picked him over Liam. If only he were in here helping, she'd be even happier. *Okay, time's up.* She needed Ty in here, repair guy or no repair guy.

The hangar was Camille's least favorite place on the ranch. She poked her head in, leaving the rest of her firmly planted outside the doors. "Hey, Ty? How much longer?"

He came over. "We've almost got it wrapped up now."

"Good, then you can be on hay detail with Emmitt. We need the dirty hay out of the barn so we can bring fresh hay in."

A befuddled look inched across his face. "I don't get the whole hay thing." She put her hands on her hips, and Ty raised his arms like she'd told him to stick 'em up. "I'm sorry, I'm sorry, I know you have very strong feelings on the subject. It's just that hay seems like hay to me."

"Thankfully, you've got me to tell you otherwise."

She hesitated, then stepped farther into the hangar and came up behind him. She put both hands on his back and tried pushing him outside. Ty didn't move. Camille pushed harder. Ty dug his heels in, crossed his arms over his chest and yawned.

Soo funny, but Camille could play dirty too. "If you don't start moving soon, I'll pinch you."

Ty gave her a look. "You stole that one from your sister. But I wouldn't mind your pinches any more than Dillon would mind hers." He looked surprised by his own words.

Camille blushed and took her hands away just in time to see Evie slip past them. *"Evie."*

She started after her daughter just as a light blue Ford pickup pulled up outside. Ty groaned. "It's Liam."

Liam? As in the guy they'd been competing against? Curiosity kicked in. Evie was watching the repairman. He didn't seem to mind. One minute in there would probably be okay. The planes weren't even running right now.

A young Sam Elliot with miles of swagger came toward them from the truck. He was wearing a wide-brimmed hat that was classic cowboy.

Ty's fingers dug into his thighs. "Liam. How's it going?"

"All right." Ty shot a look back to Liam's truck. Liam followed his gaze. "I'm alone."

Friction was too subtle a word for the waves of tension crashing around them. Camille had avoided asking Ty too much about Liam, knowing he didn't care for the subject. But now that Liam was here, she had questions.

Liam looked at her. "You must be Camille. Phoebe says amazing things."

Ty inched closer to her. "Camille, this is Liam Kendrick. He owns Bugaroo Ranch."

"Nice to meet you." She shook his hand and felt Ty tense beside her.

It was the final showdown scene from every old Western playing out in front of her. Liam and Ty faced off. They didn't have guns, but they had the hardest stares Camille had ever seen. Then Liam's broke.

"Look, I didn't come here to get into things. I just wanted to congratulate you." He held his hand out to Ty. "I'm not happy about it, but

Phoebe told me some of your ideas, and I've gotta admit they sound pretty good."

Ty looked at Liam's hand like it had tentacles, but he shook it anyway. "Thanks."

Liam sighed. "Maybe if I had a girlfriend who was a decorator too, I'd have stood a chance. Though from the way you wowed Phoebe, Camille, I still think you'd have come out the winner."

What did he just say? "I'm not Ty's girlfriend."

Liam's face blanked, then shifted back to Ty. "That so? Phoebe seems to think otherwise."

Camille blushed, but Ty backed her up. "Camille's just helping me out. It's business."

Liam stared at them. "Uh-huh." There was a long pause, then he turned and headed for his truck. "Nice meeting you, Camille."

But Ty wasn't done. "Say hi to *Mia* for me." From anyone else, it would have been a simple, friendly hello. Except nothing about the way Ty said it sounded simple. Or friendly. Maybe if his teeth hadn't been gritting together. Who was Mia anyway?

When Liam turned around, his face had aged ten years. "Mia's gone. She left."

The effect on Ty was instantaneous. Every muscle that was tensing eased up, and the lines in his forehead disappeared. "Left? You mean… for good?"

Liam nodded. "She went back to Florida."

"When?"

"A couple weeks ago."

They stood staring at each other. "I'm sorry," said Ty. This time it almost sounded like he meant it.

"Me too." It felt like the silence might never end. Liam started his truck up without another word and pulled away.

Camille needed answers before jealousy dug its nails in. *No*, not jealousy. Curiosity. That was all. "Who's Mia?"

Ty looked a little gray when he answered. "My ex-girlfriend."

Ohh. Now things made sense. "You never mentioned her."

Ty shrugged. "It was a long time ago."

"Yeah, but it might've been nice to know."

"We're just business partners, Camille. Business partners don't talk about their love lives."

A tiny dagger poked her heart. It was silly. Ty was right, they were business partners. So why did hearing him say that sting so much?

The plane started up in the hangar, and Camille's head whipped around. *Evie.* She ran inside and whisked Evie out of there before anything could happen. Evie wiggled against her, trying to get away.

The repair guy cut the engine and shouted out to Ty, "All good here."

Ty thanked him but hung back. "You know, you might not get so scared of planes if you knew something about them. I could teach you and Evie a few things. Like a mini flying lesson."

Seriously? "I thought we were just business partners. Do partners give each other flying lessons?"

"When part of your business is operating airplanes, yes." His jaw tightened.

"Absolutely not. Evie would be terrified. Look how upset she is already." Evie's eyes were watery, and her face was pink.

"If Evie's upset, it's only because you're upset."

Camille scoffed. "I'm not upset."

"The last time you said that you stormed out of here with hardly a goodbye."

"Well, I won't make that mistake again. I'll say it very clearly for you. *Goodbye*."

She led Evie away from the hangar, but the wedding was coming up fast. She couldn't go home just because Ty was behaving like a child. Instead she spent the rest of the day ignoring him and concentrating on the hay that he didn't seem to *get*.

When she tucked Evie into bed that night, Evie reached over to her nightstand and opened the top drawer. She handed Camille a picture. Only this one wasn't Milkshake and Honey. It was her and Ty. Evie was standing between them holding their hands.

A tiny sliver of guilt pricked Camille's heart. She looked at her daughter. "You really like Ty, don't you?" Evie nodded. Camille kissed her daughter's head. "Me too."

Bzzzz. Ty's phone vibrated on his nightstand. He rolled over and looked at the incoming text from Camille.

Sorry about today. Friends?

Ty didn't want to talk to her. Didn't want to admit he'd lost control of his emotions the second Liam had shown up. Learning about his breakup with Mia had only made things worse somehow, and he'd taken it out on Camille. He set his phone back on the nightstand and returned to his book.

Bzzzz.

He stared at the phone without touching it. The green light blinked, reminding him there was a message waiting…waiting…waiting. Ty put his book down and checked it.

Are you still mad?

Mad? No, he wasn't mad. Irritated, maybe. Frustrated, definitely. It was impossible not to be when dealing with Camille. His emotions were all out of whack whenever she was around, and he didn't like that. Even if he did like her.

Not "like." Appreciate. Respect.

He put the phone down again and shut off the light. *Bzzzz.* Was she gonna keep this up all night? Maybe he should just turn his phone off. Except when he picked it up to do just that, Camille's message stopped him. It wasn't a text. It was a selfie of her making the silliest, cutest face he'd ever seen.

Ty turned the light back on and sat up. He leaned against the headboard and tried to think of something to say, but everything that came out was either too saccharine or too crabby. He wanted to say he was sorry. That he admired her. That he liked spending time with her, maybe even more than he had with Mia.

Stop.

His inner voice was right. Getting too personal was a mistake, but keeping things professional was harder than he'd imagined. Better to say nothing. He went to shut the light off again when a new text came in.

I know you're awake. I can see into your room with my binoculars.

Ty got out of bed and looked out the window. His finger hovered over the keyboard.

Can you really see me? I can't see you.

He hit Send.
His screen flashed almost instantly.

OMG. Did you really look? I was totally kidding.

He grinned and sent back a text.

Sure you were.

His phone flashed again.

It would be super creepy if I was watching you. Like a stalker.

Ty thought a second.

It might be nice too. Knowing you cared enough to pay so much attention.

His screen stayed dark, and Ty kicked himself for putting one toe over the line. Nothing about his last text was professional. He waited two minutes then sent her another one.

I'm sorry for today too.

Her return message came a second later.

Apology accepted. See you tomorrow...partner.

Partner. It was definitely safer than words like *girlfriend.*

See you then. Good night.

Good night.

Ty lay back down and turned out his light. He took one last look at the selfie Camille had sent him and smiled. *Cute. Definitely cute.* When he finally turned off his phone and closed his eyes, her face didn't go dark like his screen. Her picture stayed lit until sleep finally came for him, hours later.

Chapter Eight

❧

Saturday morning started out pretty good. Camille, Evie and Nikki got to Sky High by eight o'clock, and Ty and Dillon were ready and waiting.

The rest of the vets were splitting their time between their regular chores and helping out with the wedding stuff. Phoebe's wedding was exactly two weeks from today, and Camille wanted to get started on cleaning out the stables and the smaller barns now that the main one was ready.

There was a lot going on, and Camille's nerves started jumping. Especially around ten o'clock when Ty disappeared. He was only gone a few minutes, but in that time Honey's tail swatted her in the face three times, and Camille's head developed a slow and steady ache.

"Where'd you go?" She stared at him with her arms folded.

He gave her an irritated look. "Do I need your okay to use the bathroom now too?"

"What's that supposed to mean?"

"You've been barking orders at me all morning."

"I'm just trying to get things done."

"So am I."

They glared at each other and kept their distance. Around noon Ty disappeared again. This time she spotted him coming out of the main barn. "I told you not to mess with anything in there. It's perfect right now."

"I wasn't messing with stuff. I was getting some tools."

"All your tools should've been cleared out by now."

"I forgot my hammer in there. Unless you want me to pound all those nails in with my hands."

Evie came over and they both cut the bickering down to a dull roar. Ty let out a breath. "Maybe we need a break. We've both been working pretty hard. What do you say we do something fun?"

Fun was a nice fantasy. "We don't have time for fun."

He cracked a lopsided grin. "Just call it a long lunch then."

Despite what Ty thought, Camille wasn't so stubborn that she refused to acknowledge her nerves were on edge. A long lunch might be just what she needed. "What did you have in mind?"

"I thought Evie might like to take the horses out. We could pack some sandwiches and ride up one of the shorter trails to a picnic spot."

"*Horse*back riding?" A full-blown mouse-running-across-the-room-and-jumping-on-the-chair kind of squeak came from her throat.

"I thought it would be fun."

In what world did danger equal fun?

"No way." She shook her head and felt Evie's eyes on her, already pleading. Six didn't mean naive. Evie understood perfectly well what she and Ty were debating, and she wanted to get her two cents in.

"It's completely safe, I promise. Tess is our safest pony and a real sweetie pie. Evie can have her, and you can have Honey. You've ridden her before."

"I wouldn't call what I did riding. I sat behind you and tried to hold on. You and Honey did all the work."

"I'll keep us on the easiest path."

Evie stepped closer to Ty, the two of them plotting together. She had to stand strong. Except Evie's chocolate drizzle eyes were digging their way in. She took Camille's hand and started pulling her toward the horses. Camille stopped her. "How long is the path?"

Ty shrugged. "We'll be back in an hour, hour and a half tops."

Camille tried to stop her sigh of acceptance before it came, but it was already there. "Okay, let's try it."

Ty gave them a quick riding lesson, then got them both saddled in and led them out. The horses seemed to know exactly where they were going, and the path was easy, just as Ty had promised. It went over the flattest part of the land and was clearly marked by dozens of well-tread hoofprints.

Five minutes in and Camille's muscles began to loosen. Ten minutes in and she was actually starting to enjoy herself.

Ty was riding beside her. Evie was just ahead of them, where they could keep an eye on her. Ty looked over. "I really appreciate all your help this past week. It's been nice having you around."

"Even with the squabbling?"

"Even with that."

Her heart flipped. "I've enjoyed it too." Something was gnawing on the back of her mind though. "Can I ask something about your planes?"

"Sure. What do you want to know?"

Camille pulled her words carefully. "How can you do it?"

He blinked. "What do you mean?"

She glanced at Evie, who was moving a mile an hour if that, and dropped her voice a little more. "You crashed in the ocean, right?"

Ty stiffened. "Yes."

"And your friend Jon passed away in a crash?" He nodded silently. "So how can you get in a plane day after day and keep flying after all that's happened to you?"

She really wanted to understand. Ty looked at the sky for a long minute, and she thought maybe he wouldn't answer. Then his voice came out soft but unwavering.

"For me, flying's like therapy. Jon wouldn't want me to stay grounded. Neither would George. When I fly, I honor everyone who can't any-more."

Camille could almost understand that. *Almost*.

Ty looked at her. "Can I ask *you* something now?" She nodded. "Are you really going back to Chicago after you sell the ranch?"

It was easy to answer, but not quite as easy as it should've been. "I'll admit Nebraska's nicer than I'd thought it would be, but Chicago's my home. My work is there. My house." The house she'd bought with Wesley. The one she only had two weeks to save, and here she was riding horses. The tension that had begun to ease rebuilt itself.

Ty's face tinged with pink. "Well, if we've only got a couple weeks left together, what do you think about dinner out one night? As business partners. There's a restaurant in town that's got a game room I'm sure Evie would love."

A restaurant? It was one thing eating together on the ranch. That was work. And the ice cream had been a business meal. But dinner at a restaurant? That was a date no matter how Ty spun it.

"Maybe we should go back." She slowed Honey down.

Ty slowed his horse, Pepper. "We're almost to the picnic spot."

"It doesn't matter. We need to get back. Evie's tired."

"Don't do that." The irritation in Ty's voice surprised her.

"Do what?"

"Use Evie as an excuse to run from your feelings."

Camille's mouth dropped open. "I'm not."

"Yes, you are. You've been doing it since day one."

"I don't know what you're talking about."

"I suggest going to a restaurant, and now it's Evie's nap time?" He shook his head.

"You're one to talk. What about Mia?"

Ty blanched. "What about her?"

"Is she the *real* reason you were so anxious to beat out Liam for Phoebe's wedding?"

He narrowed his eyes at her. "Mia's got nothing

to do with it." It was almost convincing. "Anyway, I don't use her to push people away."

If Ty thought Camille was gonna listen to any more of this, he was kidding himself. She gently tugged Honey's reins to the left, but instead of turning around completely, Honey took two steps off the path.

"Camille, careful."

She shot him an annoyed look. "I think we've had enough fun for today, Ty. Thanks." She tried again to move Honey in the direction she wanted to go, but Honey only moved farther off the path.

"Camille, you're twisting the reins wrong. You need to—"

Honey took three more steps away from the path then let out a whinny that made Camille jump in her saddle. A tan snake with orange splotches was playing games with Honey's feet. Honey backed up, but the snake slithered after her.

Ty's voice was urgent. "Camille, don't panic. Take Honey's reins, twist them gently toward me, and get back on the path." Evie let out a soft cry.

Camille tried to do what Ty said and steer Honey toward the path, but she couldn't take her eyes off the snake. That thing in her chest—what was it called? Oh, yeah, her heart—was beating too fast. Instead of twisting the reins, she pulled back on them. Honey reared up, and Camille barely hung on.

Evie screamed, and that only made things worse. The snake jumped forward, and Honey jumped back. She reared up again, and this time the reins slipped right through Camille's fingers and her body slipped off the saddle. Her feet searched for ground and only found air. Her arms flailed like something out of a movie. She was flying. And a second later she was crashing.

Ty moved fast. The impulse to panic lay at his feet and was creeping up to his knees. Ocean waves threatened to overtake the prairie grass, and Jon's faded outline began calling for him.

Not now.

Camille was lying on the ground in a heap. He focused on her. There was nothing else, no one else, just her and him and the space between them.

His feet hit the ground and he pulled Evie off Tess's back. "Stay here. Don't move, it's really important. Understand?"

Evie was sobbing, but not so much she couldn't follow what he said. She wiped her eyes and nodded. Ty turned and ran.

He reached Camille out of breath and sweating. She was on her side, her face hidden from his view. *Please, God, let her be okay.* The prayer

came so easily it surprised him, and then it irritated him. If this was another test, he'd never
speak to Him again.

"Camille?" He rolled her over and she groaned.
Blue eyes blinked at him, and a slender hand
touched her head.

"Am I okay?"

The pressure on Ty's shoulders lifted. "If you
can ask, you probably are." He cast a glance back
at Evie. She was standing where he'd left her.
Honey had made her own way back to the path
and was keeping guard. Camille started to sit. He
pushed her back down. "Don't move."

For the first time since he'd met her, she didn't
argue with him. "How many fingers am I holding up?"

"Two."

Good. Clear vision and no bump meant no
head trauma. It was the rest of her he was worried about.

A few scrapes on her arms were no big deal,
but her leg was another matter. Camille's left
ankle was swelling up. He could see it even under
her jeans. He pushed the pant leg up and found
a tennis ball where her ankle should have been.
He laid two fingers on it, not even pressing, and
she winced.

"You'll be okay, we just need to get some ice
on it." He said it with confidence, knowing that's

what it took to keep people from getting scared, but his insides were twisting. "I'll have Emmitt check you over back at the house."

She nodded and her eyes shifted from him to Evie. She propped herself up on her elbows and waved, trying to reassure her daughter everything was okay. Evie started running toward them.

"No!" Camille shouted and tried jumping to her feet. Ty set one hand on her shoulder and pushed her down again. "Evie, stay there." She stopped running. Camille looked at him. "Where's the snake?"

"Gone. It wasn't dangerous anyway. Just a rat snake."

If Camille hadn't panicked, Honey wouldn't have panicked either and the snake probably wouldn't have bothered them. But he didn't say that out loud; it sounded too much like blame. This wasn't Camille's fault. Ty's gut clenched. The second she'd gotten off the path, he should've gone after her.

"Come on, let's get you up." Ty put one arm around her waist and his other under her knees, careful not to jostle her as he lifted her off the ground.

Honey was chewing on some grass. She looked up when they came over, whinnied lightly, then pressed her muzzle to Camille's hand, her way of apologizing. Camille wasn't quite ready for forgiveness.

Evie grabbed ahold of Camille. She was small, but when she was scared, her muscles turned all bodybuilder. His grip on Camille tightened as they hugged each other. When they let go, he started lifting Camille toward Honey's saddle. Her eyes widened and she shook her head. "No way."

"You can't walk back. We're over a mile out."

Camille's lips tightened and her resolve deepened. But if he carried her back, he'd end up jostling her more than Honey, and the faster they got back, the faster they could ice that ankle.

"You can ride with me. I'll tie Honey's reins to Pepper's so she doesn't stray."

Camille's eyes shifted to the black horse Ty had been riding. "Okay."

He gently placed her in the saddle. When she was secure, he turned to Evie. He went to hoist her back up on Tess, but she screamed and wiggled out of his grip like she was part cat.

"Evie, sweetie, everything's okay. We've gotta go back." He stroked Tess's muzzle, but Evie wouldn't budge. In the two seconds it had taken for Honey to throw Camille, Evie had decided all horses couldn't be trusted.

Camille's ankle was still swelling, and her face

was a little pale. Something had to give. His mind searched for the right thing to say.

"Evie, your mom's gonna be all right, but she needs to see a doctor. Emmitt's like a doctor for the army, but he's back at the house. We need to get her there."

Distrust crept into Evie's eyes.

"Honey's not a bad horse, she just got scared. Just like your mom…er, *you*…get scared of planes. Only Honey's scared of snakes." Evie looked at Honey again, and the distrust flickered out. It was replaced with something else—empathy? She pointed to Tess.

Ty thought he understood. "Tess is scared of snakes too—most horses are—but I'm right here with you, and so is God. We'll keep you safe." His words came out of nowhere, surprising him.

A Bible verse Jon used to love quoting flashed through his mind. "God says He's always there with us when we're lost or scared. 'For I the Lord thy God, will hold thy right hand, saying unto thee, Fear not. I will help thee.'"

Evie was staring at him, and he wondered if he'd made a mistake. Did Evie even know about God? He'd never thought to ask Camille. But her hand reached out and took hold of his, and her eyes steeled. She took a step toward Tess.

He waited a moment to see if she might change her mind, then he lifted her up. Tess stood perfectly still, and Evie reached out and touched her neck, stroking her gently. Ty didn't have time to overthink what had just happened. He got them moving.

Camille knew Ty was being as gentle as he could, but when he laid her on the couch, the pain in her ankle broke the ten-point scale and jumped all the way to a hundred. At least it cleared the fog from her vision. The only thing that stopped her from crying out was Evie. Her daughter was already scared enough, and there was no way she was adding to it.

Time for a brave face. This was where expertise and motherhood came together. She'd been using brave faces since Wesley's death and considered herself a master of disguise.

Deep breath, big smile. She took Evie's hand and gave it a squeeze. "Don't worry, sweetie, I'm fine. It hardly even hurts." Her smile stretched from ear to ear. Evie blinked, not fooled for a second. Maybe her brave face wasn't what it used to be.

Dillon ran over. "What happened?" He was already kneeling down to take a look.

"Camille got thrown."

Alarm hit Dillon's eyes. "I'll find Emmitt." He ran outside.

Ty grabbed a pillow and propped it under Camille's head. "Is that okay?" She nodded, and he brushed a strand of hair from her face. The warmth she so often saw in his eyes radiated all the way down to his fingertips. He took her right hand and gave it a squeeze. Evie was standing off to the side, looking terrified.

"Hey, Evie," Ty said. "What do you call a sleeping dinosaur? A dino-*snore*." Evie did not giggle, but her tears slowed. "Why did the student eat their homework? Because their teacher said it was a piece of cake."

Camille groaned and moved her leg without meaning to. Her ankle cried out. She crushed Ty's hand. He let her. "Are you sure I don't need a hospital? I mean, can Emmitt handle this?"

Ty smiled. "Emmitt was 18 Delta."

A special forces medic? They were the best in the world. Wesley had always held them in high regard. George too. Any doubts she had vanished.

The front door flew open. Dillon and Emmitt ran into the room. Emmitt saw Camille on the couch and hurried over. "Ty, out of the way." It was brisk, but he was probably used to giving orders at critical times.

Ty immediately made room for him, but he didn't let go of her hand. Emmitt kneeled down and started examining Camille's swollen ankle. Two fingers pressed against it. The hiss of air that ran through her teeth was pure reflex. Evie's tears started up again.

Emmitt stayed calm. "Evie, I'm gonna make your mommy feel better, but to do that I need your help. Think you can help me?" Evie nodded. "Good. I need you to wrap some ice in a dish towel for me. Make sure the ice doesn't fall out, okay? It's real important." She nodded again, and Emmitt's eyes shifted to Dillon. "Let her do it, and bring me some orange juice."

Dillon didn't question him. He took Evie's hand and led her into the kitchen.

Camille held her breath. "How bad is it?"

Emmitt offered a reassuring smile. "You're gonna be fine."

Fine? That was the word people used when the kitchen was about to explode and they didn't want anyone to panic. It was a mom answer.

More pillows came off the couch and made their way under Camille's leg, propping it up. "Does it hurt anywhere else?" Emmitt asked.

"No."

He checked her over anyway, making sure. "Do you want the good news or the bad news?"

"Surprise me."

"Nothing's broken. It's just sprained."

She could live with that. "So, what's the bad news?"

"You're gonna need crutches. Maybe just a couple days, maybe a week."

Crutches? Seriously? She had a six-year-old to take care of and a wedding to finish planning. "No way. Can't I just ice it?"

The look on Emmitt's face was practiced patience. A doctor explaining physics to a third grader. "The ice will bring the swelling down, but it won't fix things. Only time and rest can do that." He stood up. "I'll be right back."

Ty's hand locked around hers. "You're doing great."

Emmitt returned a minute later holding the infamous crutches and a fuzzy purple thing. He set the purple thing aside and leaned the crutches against the wall. They stood sentinel over her.

Dillon and Evie returned. A large lumpy dish towel was in her daughter's hands. She held it out to Emmitt, waiting for his approval. She wasn't crying anymore, but her eyes were still red and watery.

"That's perfect, Evie. Good job." Emmitt placed the towel on Camille's ankle. He handed her two pills along with the orange juice Dillon had brought in. "They're anti-inflammatories. Two now, two before bed. It'll help with the swelling."

She swallowed them back and set the orange juice aside. The fuzzy purple thing was back in

Emmitt's hand. He kneeled down to Evie's level and held it out to her. Camille finally saw the long trunk, and the fuzzy purple thing took shape. Evie loved elephants.

Emmitt cleared his throat and his cheeks turned pink. "I thought you might like this. Her name is Mrs. Snugglesworth, but I guess you can call her anything you want. She was mine when I was little, and she makes me feel better when I'm scared."

The last of Evie's tears evaporated. One hand reached out and grabbed the elephant, holding it close. She wrapped her arms around Emmitt's neck, pulling him into a hug.

Camille was glad Evie's tears were gone, because hers were just about to start. How could she finish Phoebe's wedding when she was stuck on crutches? Ty still had hold of her hand and must have tapped into what she was thinking.

"Don't worry about Phoebe's wedding. You can give the orders, and we'll follow them." Emmitt and Dillon nodded. "I'll round everybody up tonight and tell them from now on it's all hands on deck."

Camille's bottom lip trembled. "But you hate taking orders."

Ty grinned. "From you, I don't mind so much."

Dillon cleared his throat. "I'm starving. Why don't we get some snacks together? Evie, Emmitt, can you help me?" The three of them left the room.

Ty was still clutching her hand in his. Eyes like a desert sunset looked back at her, and her heart forgot how to beat. "Maybe that restaurant you mentioned wasn't such a bad idea. I might be off the crutches by next Saturday."

"Saturday is date night," he said.

She blushed and fought the urge to pull her hand away. "I don't date pilots, but I suppose I can be friends with one. Business partners can be friends too, can't they?"

"Sure they can." He squeezed her hand, and she squeezed back.

Friends. She tried the word on, and it fit nicely. Who couldn't use another friend in their life?

Chapter Nine

꧂

Evie held Mrs. Snugglesworth close as they entered the church. Camille spotted Ty waving to them from up front and smoothed down her dress, almost losing one of her crutches in the process. Nikki caught it before it could fall and leaned over. "Why are you so nervous? Ty's already seen you at your worst."

Camille glared at her. "When's the last time you were in a church?" Nikki shrugged. "Exactly. Let's make a good first impression."

"I'm pretty sure God doesn't need first impressions. He kind of made us. He already knows what we're all about."

Camille shook her head. "Just be good."

"Well, there's a first time for everything."

The entire team at Sky High took up the first three pews. There were three open spots on Ty's right. They slid in and she almost dropped her crutch again. Why *was* she so nervous? A check-list of reasons formed in her head.

One, Ty was already reaching for her hand. Two, Avery was probably definitely absolutely lurking around there somewhere. Three, if any-one could see through all her brave faces and false smiles, it was God. And even though she talked to Him every now and again, it wasn't quite the same as a face-to-face.

"Hi," Ty whispered.

"Hi." She squeezed his hand, then let it go, not sure if hand-holding was church appropriate. Or friend appropriate.

Dillon and Nikki were flashing smiles at each other from across the pew. Maricela and Josh had their heads together. There was just one person missing.

"Where's Emmitt?"

A worried crease formed between Ty's eyes. "Back at the ranch."

"Is he sick?"

"Not exactly."

"So, what's wrong?"

There was a five-second hesitation, which was five seconds longer than Ty normally gave. "He's just not up for church today."

Something wasn't right. Time for her mom voice. One word, single syllable, drawn out. *"Ty..."*

He looked over as she arched her eyebrow extra high. "I think Emmitt's in trouble."

Motherly instincts immediately kicked in. Step one: ascertain the problem. Step two: figure out how to fix it. Step three: fix it. "Trouble how?"

"Remember when I said Dillon and I missed George's funeral because we were helping out one of the vets?" She nodded. "Well, it was Emmitt."

She opened her mouth to question him further, but the minister stepped out and began speaking. She made a mental note to get back to Emmitt later, then shot Evie a look, worried what her daughter would think about all this. They hadn't been to church in years. Evie probably didn't even remember going with Wesley.

The minister was on the younger side of middle-aged, and the top of his head was just starting to bald. The crinkly look at the corners of his eyes reminded her of Santa Claus. If he'd been rounder in the frame and had a white beard, he probably could have pulled it off.

Camille wasn't sure just how much Evie really understood, but her eyes never left the minister. When it was all over, they exited the church and Evie's eyes were glowing.

"Like it?" Nikki asked, taking Evie's hand. Evie nodded. When the minister came out, she gave him a hug. She was full of them this week.

The minister laughed, and the Santa Claus–effect became that much more real.

Ty addressed the minister. "I guess you've met Evie. This is Minister Powell." He introduced them all, and the minister shook their hands. Nikki told him what a wonderful sermon it had been, and Evie nodded her agreement. The glow didn't leave her eyes.

If this was the effect church had on Evie, then they'd definitely be coming more often. If only God could get her to talk again or even smile, she might finally forgive Him for all that He'd put her through the last couple years.

Ty tapped her on the shoulder, and she spun so fast the crutch slipped out from under her again. She pitched forward. Ty caught her, then he caught her crutch. Their eyes locked, and for one moment she thought he might not let go. Then he righted her, and she was free from his grip. It left an empty feeling inside her.

"We're having breakfast back at Sky High. You and Evie interested? Nikki's welcome too, of course."

The pitter-patter of her heart moved from a slow Sunday drive to racetrack speed. "Sounds fun." They could eat, then get some work in.

"I can give you a ride back, if you want. I'm sure Dillon wouldn't mind riding with Nikki, if she's okay with that."

"Just let me check." Nikki was fine with driving Buffy back to the ranch, and Dillon was thrilled to accompany her.

She and Ty got Evie buckled in, and Camille was about to get back to the Emmitt thing when Avery appeared from nowhere. "Hi." She gave Ty a hug, then gave Camille one too. She flipped her hair back over her shoulder and giggled. Camille knew what giggles like that meant—the triple *F* threat. *Fun, friendly, flirty.*

"Are you joining us for breakfast?" Camille hoped her words didn't sound as jealous out loud as they did in her head.

Avery hesitated. "I'd love to, but I probably shouldn't."

Camille disguised relief with a smile she wished was genuine. Neither Avery nor Ty seemed to catch her underlying anxiety slash jealousy slash silliness. That was probably a good thing. She'd already shown Ty enough crazy; she didn't need him seeing any more.

Avery chatted them up a few minutes, then went to meet some friends. As soon as she was gone, Camille felt a load lift from her shoulders. She knew it was silly, but that didn't make her feelings any less real, or any easier to deal with.

Ty parked his truck in the driveway and helped Camille out. Mini donuts and coffee cake were already laid out on the dining table. A few bites and Evie would be on a morning sugar high; a few more and it would carry her straight through to the afternoon.

"Don't worry, we've got more than sugar," Ty said, reading her thoughts. "And vegetarian options." Camille smiled.

About half the group had beaten them back. The other half were still on their way. Dillon and Nikki were among the missing. Chairs were filling up quickly. Ty grabbed three together and pulled one out for her. Camille managed to hang on to her crutches as she sat down.

The kitchen had one of those wooden swing doors. It was a little bit old-fashioned but added a touch of charm to the place. Maricela pushed it open from the other side, almost knocking into the back of Ty's head. She looked worried. "Ty, we've got a problem. It's Emmitt."

Camille had never seen the look on a pilot's face when he was crashing, but she imagined it looked something like Ty's at this moment. He rushed into the kitchen without a word. Camille hesitated, then went after him. If something was wrong with Emmitt, she wanted to help.

Emmitt was standing next to the island. His back was to them, and he looked okay from what she could see. Nothing was bleeding. Nothing was burning. If he'd had an accident while cooking, wouldn't there be some sign? Black smoke or singed hair or a dropped knife?

Ty was standing just ahead of her. "Emmitt." His voice was low and steady.

Slowly Emmitt turned around. For half a second she thought she was looking at a different person. This wasn't the same man who'd worked on her ankle just yesterday. The one who'd known how to console Evie and given orders with confidence and grace.

Emmitt's face was pale. A thin film of sweat covered his brow. His right hand clutched a can of unopened beer. It was shaking. It wasn't a look she'd seen before, but she knew what it meant just the same. It was the face of someone struggling with addiction.

When Ty spoke again, it was without judgment. "Emmitt, let's talk through this, okay?"

Maricela, Josh and several others were standing just behind her. She caught their ashen faces and knew this was bad. Things started clicking into place. Emmitt's silence, his moodiness, his intensity.

Emmitt shook his head and his entire face crinkled. "I can't. It's just too hard." His voice cracked, and he popped the lid off the beer.

Maricela was biting her lip. Ty looked ready to tackle Emmitt if the can moved even an inch toward his mouth.

Soft footsteps came forward from the back of the room, and Evie appeared. She walked toward Emmitt. Camille moved to stop her, but something made her pause. Evie was holding the purple elephant Emmitt had given her.

Emmitt did not look up at her approach, so Evie reached out and tugged on his sleeve. He glanced at her, and she held out Mrs. Snugglesworth. He stared at it a moment, and when he made no move to take it, Evie took his free hand and placed the elephant in it for him. Then she wrapped her arms around his waist and gave him a hug.

No one spoke. No one moved. It was a full minute before Evie pulled away, and then she didn't leave his side. Emmitt squeezed the elephant and held it close to his chest. A smile so soft it was almost undetectable emerged on his face. Evie's eyes never left his, and when he tried to hand Mrs. Snugglesworth back, Evie pushed it toward him again and shook her head.

Emmitt took a breath. "Thank you, Evie. This means a lot."

She gave him another hug, and this time when she let go, he squeezed the elephant and walked around the island to the sink. The can of beer hung over the drain for a moment, then Emmitt tipped it upside down and amber liquid poured out. He crushed the can up, put it in the recycling bin and took Evie's hand. "Why don't we eat?"

Ty was freaking out. He piled his plate high with bacon, eggs and toast. Going through the motions was easy; he'd done it a thousand times before. He laughed where appropriate and spoke when expected to, and the second he thought he could leave the table without drawing attention, he did.

The cows looked up as he went into the dairy barn. Several long moos greeted him before falling silent. They understood alone time. It was one of the things he appreciated most about them.

He sat down on a hay bale, stood up, sat back down. Finally, his feet carried him over to the stalls and he stroked the tips of Milkshake's ears. She always liked that. When he walked away from her, she mooed her disapproval. Ty didn't blame her; he disapproved of himself sometimes.

The roof was hiding the sky, but that didn't matter. God saw through everything. Ty looked up at it. "What do you want from me?" There was no answer, as usual, but this time Ty thought he already knew.

Time to stop being scared.

The barn doors squeaked open. He didn't have to look up to know who was there. Crutches were a one-of-a-kind sound. He turned and saw Camille standing there, the only person who wasn't an intrusion.

"Hi." She hesitated before taking another step toward him. "Are you okay?"

A million thoughts ran through his mind, but one was clear above all the others. *Tell her how you feel. Do it now, before you waste any more time.*

But was Ty even sure of his feelings? He'd been sure about Mia too. And look what happened.

"I'm okay." Maybe he answered too fast, or maybe Camille was just that good at picking out lies. Either way, she didn't buy it for a second.

"Is this about Emmitt?"

How was he supposed to answer that? "No. Yes. Both, I guess." *Just be honest. With her and with yourself.* "It's more about Evie than Emmitt, I think."

"Evie? What about her?"

Ty didn't know where to start. He moved a hay bale over so she could sit down, then took the one next to her. "I go to church every week, but for the last few years I've just been going through the motions. God and I, we had a bit of a falling out after my crash."

She laid one hand on his arm. "I'm sure it was hard. Being stuck out in the ocean alone like that—"

"I wasn't alone."

"Sure, of course. God is always with us."

"That's not what I meant. It wasn't just me on that plane." He drew in a breath. "Jon was there too."

Periwinkle flickered beneath the deep blue of her eyes. "Oh."

His heart wasn't racing; it was moving ultra-slow, gripped by a crushing hand that made it hard to breathe. "I don't talk about it. Much." He had at first, but only because he'd had to. There'd been questions and he'd had to give answers. Especially to Jon's family.

"Ty, I'm sorry."

No one would ever be as sorry as he was. "I tried to get him out of the plane, but the storm was too intense. The water kept rushing in. By the time I finally got him free, it was too late." The medics had told him later that Jon would probably have died anyway. His internal injuries had been massive.

If they hadn't used that word—*probably*—Ty might've been able to forgive himself years earlier.

"Ty, you don't have to—"

"No, I need to say this." His fingers curled around hers. "When I got home after that, I was different. Mia sensed it, but I refused to see it. I did what I accused you of doing the other day. I pushed her away."

There were no judgments or I-told-you-sos from Camille. She just squeezed his hand harder. "Mia left me for Liam, but it wasn't her fault. I was scared to let anyone get close. Losing Jon hurt, and I never wanted to hurt like that again."

It was weird saying all that out loud. Admitting to himself what he'd known deep down. They sat silently for a minute. Ty had already opened up to Camille more than anyone else in the last four years. And now that he'd started, he didn't want to stop.

"I thought God had abandoned me, and today I was proven wrong."

Confused wrinkles formed around Camille's eyes. "What does Evie have to do with that?"

"I've spent the last two years trying to help Emmitt, and today I couldn't. But Evie…" He shook his head. "God was in that kitchen with us, working through her. I felt it. He's always been here, all this time. I just didn't know it until today."

She looked at him. "I think I felt it too. When Evie came into the kitchen, I went to stop her, but something told me not to."

Okay. Time to tell her how he felt. No more fear. No more running.

"Look, Camille… I like you. A lot. Not just as business partners. And not just as friends."

She looked down where her right hand was interlocked with his, her left hand carefully at her side.

"I don't—"

"Just listen." He tipped her chin back so their eyes met. "I don't care how little time we have together. I don't want to waste it."

Her hands came up behind his neck. She was breathing hard. Ty moved in closer, and when she didn't pull away, he closed the space between them. Her kiss was soft and warm and so much better than he'd imagined.

A summer wind stirred inside him, blowing soft scents and happy thoughts through his mind and body. He couldn't remember the last time he'd felt so alive.

Then the barn doors opened, and a woman's voice jumped out at them. "Oh."

Camille pulled away, and Ty turned to see Nikki and Dillon standing there. They both looked shocked. "I'm sorry." Nikki started shooing Dillon out the door, but Camille was already on her feet.

Ty saw the panic on her face and knew she was about to bolt. "Camille, wait." But she was already moving. Her crutches carried her out the door without a word.

* * *

Camille put on Evie's favorite cartoon to keep her occupied, then hurried upstairs, almost falling down when her crutches slipped. She shut the bedroom door behind her. Nikki opened it a second later.

"Not now." But her sister only stood there, grinning.

"You've gotta be kidding. I need details." But Camille shot her a look, and Nikki's grin dropped off her face. "What's wrong?"

Her sister was oblivious sometimes. "Do you really need to ask me that?"

She sat on the edge of her bed, unsuccessfully pushing back her tears. Nikki stayed where she was a minute, then sat down beside her.

"This is about Wesley, isn't it?"

Camille shook her head. "No, it's about Ty." She couldn't look at Nikki. She couldn't face the judgment that had to be there.

"Yeah, but isn't Wesley kind of wrapped up in all that?"

Camille looked at her, and it wasn't judgment she saw, only concern. "No. My feelings for Wesley haven't changed, and they won't. Ever. He's my husband."

"And what's Ty?"

There was no good way to answer that. "He's my friend."

"Is that all?"

Camille shrugged and stared at her feet. "Ty wants more than I can give."

Nikki hesitated. "It looked like you were giving plenty back in the barn." Camille shot her a look. "I just mean it didn't exactly look like you minded what was happening."

Camille's insides twisted. "Evie doesn't need another pilot in her life."

But Nikki wasn't ready to let this drop. "This is about you and Ty, not Evie. Stop using her as your excuse."

Nikki's words slapped her across the face. They mirrored Ty's words from the other day so closely that she didn't know what to say, or how to avoid the truth behind them.

"So what if I like him? *So what?* We're leaving here in less than two weeks, and it's not like Ty's going with us. This can never work."

Nikki's silence was more unsettling than her constant questions. "Have you tried praying about it?"

Praying? George's Bible was in the nightstand, but she hadn't even cracked it open. Nikki obviously took her silence as a no.

"Maybe you should try. Just because you don't have the answers, doesn't mean God won't have them."

"Prayers didn't help Wesley. And they haven't helped Evie."

Her words hung in the air. Nikki sat there a minute, then squeezed Camille's hand and stood up. "Just promise me that before you do anything rash, like throw away a potentially amazing relationship because you're scared, you'll give God a chance."

Camille met Nikki's eyes. "Will you stop harassing me about Ty if I promise?"

"Yes."

"Then I promise." Nikki left the room, and Camille lay back. She'd promised to pray but hadn't said when. Right now all she wanted to do was pretend she was back in her home in the city, and her heart wasn't being torn in a million different directions.

Chapter Ten

Barns? Check. Stables? Check again. Hangar? Camille was saving that for last. Her plan there was simple. Ty would move all the planes out so the band could set up and the whole thing would turn into one big dance floor. They'd string some lights from the ceiling, add flowers and a few extra touches, and it would look spectacular.

For now she just wanted to focus on the space where the ceremony would be held. Early this morning Phoebe had decided definitively upon the stables. She and Brett would both be on horseback when they said their vows.

The ground here was hilly and rocky. Camille had to figure out how to set up a couple hundred chairs without them all tipping over. And she had to do it while balancing on these crutches. Too bad Nikki was home waiting for some buyers, or Camille could make her pick up all these rocks and help clear the ground.

Josh and Maricela finished spray-painting the mason jars and held one out for her inspection. The mirror spray paint gave off an ultra-glossy finish that looked cool with the LED candle flames. "Perfect." Josh grinned and they went to join Evie and the others who were busy stringing up clotheslines.

Ty spotted her from over by the hangar and made a beeline in her direction. Camille realized she'd left her water bottle in the dairy barn and hurried to get it. Ty followed her. The crutches were slowing her down.

Now that she thought about it, she could get fresh water from inside the house. And ice. Way better than a lukewarm water bottle. She went in through the front door and shut it behind her. A minute later it opened and closed again.

There was a back door that led out of the kitchen and into the yard where a good-sized garden grew fruits and veggies. She went out the door but wasn't fast enough. Ty's hand landed on her shoulder.

"Camille, will you wait a second?"

She turned to face him, already blushing and hating herself for it. Blushing meant he was getting to her, and Ty was definitely not getting to her. "Did you need something?"

The innocence in her voice didn't fool him.

"You've been avoiding me for two days. Don't you think it's time we talked?"

"I'm not avoiding you. I've been right here."

"Every time I get close, you run away. Just give me a minute. *One minute.*"

Camille sighed. "Okay, fine. One minute."

Ty ran a hand through his hair. "I'm sorry I kissed you. I shouldn't have done that."

She'd expected him to defend their kiss, to try to convince her it had been the right thing to do. She was relieved when he didn't. *Mostly.* The tiniest corner of her heart dipped a toe into disappointment.

"Okay then." She didn't know what else to say.

"Do you think we can just forget it and go back to being friends?"

Easier said than done. "I don't know." How could she forget a kiss like that? She'd never admit to sparks, but there had definitely been flickers.

"I miss your dimples," he said. "I miss our talks. I miss *you.* So, if it comes down to being friends or being nothing, I'll take friends."

That was sweet, and difficult to argue with. "I don't have dimples."

Ty grinned. "Trust me. Dimples and you are kind of an item."

Her heart started pitter-pattering. She told it

to settle down but couldn't help the giggle that floated out of her.

"See, there they are." Ty reached for her hand, but she pulled it back.

"Do friends usually hold hands? Do you hold hands with Emmitt? Or Dillon?"

He hesitated. "No." There was an awkward pause. "Okay. What about dinner? Friends have dinner together, don't they?"

She wasn't gonna let him reason his way into her heart though. "Yes, but I'm not sure that's a good idea anymore. Dinners are too—" *Dangerous? Exciting?* "—romantic."

A U-shaped crinkle tugged the skin between his eyes. It only lasted a minute, then his face brightened. "What if it wasn't dinner? What if it was the least romantic thing possible?"

She tilted her head to the side. "Like what?"

His eyes danced around as a smile spread across his face. "Bugs."

Bugs? Like...bugs?

"The nature center is hosting Bug Fest this Saturday. Hundreds of bugs from all over the world. You get to see them up close and even touch them. They do it every summer."

Ew. Even ladybugs grossed her out. "I don't know about that."

"You've gotta admit there's nothing romantic

about it. Plus, there will be tons of kids there. Not exactly date night."

He had her there. "I don't know if we've got time for something like that."

"Just a couple hours."

"Like the horseback riding?" She arched an eyebrow.

"The nature center doesn't even have horses, and it's only a mile or two from here. You can almost see it from the ranch. And we've got things pretty under control here, don't you think?"

He had a point. The last couple days Ty and everyone here had been true to their word and really pitched in.

"They open at eight. I can pick you up at your place, we'll go check it out, then come straight here and get to work."

She tried to picture Evie petting a giant cockroach and her stomach churned. But giant cockroaches were probably safer than horses or anything else around here. "Evie might actually get a kick out of it."

"That's a yes?"

"That's a yes."

His lopsided smile spread, and Camille's heart fluttered. She started to wobble on her crutches and realized she'd been on her feet way too long. Ty helped her over to a bench. "Do you need anything?"

"I'm fine. My ankle's back to normal size now, it just starts to ache after a little while."

"You're sure?"

She never had gotten her water. "Actually, a drink would be nice."

"Coming right up."

He went inside, and Camille relaxed. She was glad they'd made up. She'd hated avoiding him the last two days. He was right, it was much better being friends than being nothing.

Her phone buzzed and she looked down at Nikki's incoming message.

We got an offer! Tell Ty. We can sign the papers this week.

Camille's throat went dry. When Ty returned with her drink, she swallowed the water in two giant gulps. "I guess you were thirsty. Want some more?" But she shook her head. Water wouldn't help right now. He was looking closely at her. "Something wrong? You look a little flush."

She forced a smile and brightened her voice. "Nope. Want to help me figure out the chairs?"

"Sure."

She stood up, and they started for the stables.

Dillon came into the hangar. "We got a booking for Saturday."

Ty looked over from inside the Piper Cub. "Flying lesson?"

"Yep. Said she heard Phoebe Saylor was getting married here and wants to see the place. She's getting married next year and thought it might be fun to jump out of a plane after they say their I dos."

Skydiving? Huh. Ty wasn't a certified instructor, but Josh had been a parachutist. He wondered how hard it would be for Josh to get certified, or if he'd even want to. He added that to his back-burner list.

"Maybe things will finally start picking up again," said Dillon. They'd had only one lesson all last week.

"If she asks, tell her we can work out the sky-diving thing." Ty would figure something out. He always did.

When Dillon didn't respond, Ty glanced over at him. He was standing with a strange expression on his face. "Have you seen Camille today?"

"Yeah, she's in the house. I told her we should probably spruce things up inside too, in case one of the guests wants to use an actual bathroom instead of those fancy porta potties. Why?"

Dillon shrugged. "No reason. It's just that I talked to Nikki and…" He put his hands in his pockets and bounced on his feet.

Ty leaned out of the plane and looked at him. "What?"

Dill didn't normally fidget. "Bug Fest, huh?

How very *un*romantic of you." He broke into a grin and the fidgeting eased.

"Unromantic was kind of the point."

"Yeah, well, there's unromantic, and then there's no-chance-in-the-world. It's a whole other level of unromantic I didn't even know existed until I heard about your Bug Fest idea."

Ty groaned. The matchmaker in Dillon just couldn't help himself, could he? "Is that it?" If all Dill wanted to do was tease him about Camille, Ty had better things to do.

There was a brief pause. Totally unnatural for Dillon's blabbermouth. "I ran into Liam yesterday."

Oh, great. No wonder Dill was acting strangely. "He told you about Mia?"

Dill nodded. He waited for Ty to say something, but Ty had nothing to say. "I'm fine." He really was too. He realized now that Mia wasn't to blame. It takes two to end a relationship. Anyway, Mia was gone, but Camille was still here. There was still time.

"So, Mia has nothing to do with choosing Bug Fest over dinner?"

"Camille liked the Bug Fest idea. It'll be fun for Evie."

Dillon shrugged. "I'm just doing my duty as your younger brother and pointing out all your mistakes. Isn't that what we're for?" Ty threw a rag at him, and Dillon ran out of the barn.

What would Dill say if he pointed out that Camille and Nikki were *both* leaving Sweetheart when this wedding was over? He suspected Dillon wouldn't like it any more than he did. When Camille walked into the hangar, he kicked his thousand-watt smile up to full volume.

"Hey." He jumped out of the Piper to greet her.

Evie was with her. She started moving toward the plane, but Camille pulled her back. She had that frantic look on her face.

"I need your help in the house. Some of the lights I put up won't turn on, and I can't figure out what's wrong with them." Her fingernails were bitten all the way down, and it looked like she'd started in on the skin around them.

"You checked the bulbs?"

"All two thousand of them."

Two thousand? No wonder she was so jittery. Evie tried to get away again, but Camille kept a firm grip. It was easier now that her crutches were gone, though he noticed she was still balancing most of her weight on one foot.

"Everyone's disappeared. I can't find Dillon, Emmitt, Maricela…" She started counting people off on her fingers. Evie finally managed to scoot away from her. "I knew you were in here fiddling with that plane again. Can you *please* help me?"

"I think everyone's just running around playing catch up." Wednesday had always been catch-up day for them, and with so much work going into the wedding, some of the normal ranch stuff had slipped past them.

"Yeah, but the wedding's in a week and a half, and we need lights that work." Here came the shuffle he'd grown so used to. Left foot, right foot, repeat. Followed by a few twists of her wedding ring.

Ty told himself it didn't matter that she still wore it. They were just friends after all. But his heart strained on the next few beats. "Just give me a minute, okay? I promise we'll get the lights working."

"Today?"

"Today."

She nodded, relieved, then turned her eyes toward the plane. Her mouth dropped open and her eyes blew up like balloons. *"Evie!"*

Ty turned and saw Evie trying to climb into the plane. She was halfway up.

Camille rushed over and pulled Evie down, but Evie wiggled free and tried to go back up. Camille pulled her into a hug so tight there was no escape. "What are you doing? Don't you know planes are dangerous?"

Ty didn't bother pointing out that this plane was safely on the ground and completely turned off. It was no more dangerous right now than a loaf of bread. None of that would matter to Camille. All she'd ever be able to see was the big bad plane, and the big bad pilot who made it fly.

Camille relaxed her grip, and Evie pointed to the plane. When Camille did not give the response Evie was hoping for, she took Ty's hand and tried pulling him toward it.

"Evie, hang on a second." Ty kneeled down so that she didn't have to look up at him. In her eyes was a look he'd seen before in his own reflection. A combination of curiosity and longing. "Do you want to go up in the plane?" Evie nodded, and a hint of desperation flashed behind the curiosity. This wasn't just something Evie *wanted* to do; it was something she *needed* to do.

But Camille was already shaking her head. "Absolutely not."

The smart play would be to back Camille up, but maybe this wasn't just about Camille. Maybe God had sent Evie here for a reason. Now the rest was up to him. He stood and faced Camille, holding on to Evie's hand so she didn't go running off.

It went against all his instincts, but if he and God were friends again, he was ready to put his trust in Him. "You and I are friends, right?" Ty asked.

Camille blinked. "Yes…"

"So as your friend, I'm telling you that right

here, in this hangar, this plane is safe. And even if you're still scared of it, Evie clearly isn't. If she wants to sit in it for a minute, don't you owe it to her to let her try?"

He knew he was asking for a fight, but Camille's bottom lip began to quiver. She looked at Evie. "I just don't understand. Evie, sweetie, do you *really* want to go in the plane?" Evie nodded. Camille's voice trembled. "But…why?"

Evie kept her silence, but Ty thought he might be able to help. He dropped Evie's hand and went over to Camille, locking eyes with her. "Do you remember when I told you that I keep flying to honor those who can't anymore?" She nodded. "Well, maybe this is Evie's way of honoring her father. Of keeping him close to her heart."

A tiny light went off in Camille's eyes. Her hands started shaking, and she swallowed three times before she said anything. "Okay. Evie, if you really want to sit in the plane, you can." Her voice cracked on the last word. She grabbed Ty's hand and squeezed it hard. "Don't turn it on. Don't let her fall."

"I promise she'll be okay." He squeezed her hand back, and Camille gave him a nod. He turned to Evie. "Okay, up we go." He lifted her into the plane, putting her right in the pilot's seat.

Evie sat there, pushing the buttons and twisting the control wheel. Camille looked ready to faint. "Don't worry, the key's not in it."

Evie touched everything. She couldn't stop. When she turned back to them, the biggest smile Ty had ever seen stretched across her face. It lit up her eyes like there were spotlights shining out of them.

Ty turned to gauge Camille's reaction, and his heart almost stopped. Her mouth was hanging open, and her face had gone completely white. Ty rushed to her side and put his arm around her waist. Camille whispered to him. "I need air."

Evie was fine where she was, lost in a world of her own. He walked Camille to the hangar doors, and she leaned against the wall sucking in air. He still had a clear view of Evie from here. If she started to climb down, he could get to her in a second.

"Are you okay?" He was worried about the way Camille's whole body seemed to be shaking. He kept one hand on her just in case her knees buckled. She was watching Evie, and then before he even realized what was happening, she was kissing him.

Camille had been fighting the urge to kiss Ty since the last time. She'd tried to convince herself she didn't need the warmth of his breath or the comfort of his lips, but she'd done a terrible job of it. This kiss now was only proof of that.

She pulled away and saw the surprised look on Ty's face. She'd surprised herself too. Evie turned and waved to them, her grin still firmly in check. That long-lost grin Camille had almost given up on, even if she'd told herself she hadn't.

"I don't know what to say." She heard the cracks in her voice and thought maybe they'd always been there; she'd just done a good job of covering them up until now.

"Neither do I." Ty was shaking a little. "What happened to being friends?"

How did she explain everything going through her head without sounding ridiculous? For two years she'd been trying to get Evie to smile, and for two years she'd failed. It turned out that Evie's smile had been there the whole time; it just needed the right person to bring it out. And that person was Ty.

"I've been waiting two years for Evie to smile again. And thanks to you, she has. I can't tell you how grateful I am."

Ty frowned. Not quite the reaction she was hoping for. "Camille, my feelings for you haven't changed, but I don't want you to kiss me because you're grateful. Or because you think you owe me something."

She was messing this up. Camille put her hands

on his shoulders, afraid he'd walk away before she could get everything out. "That's not why I kissed you." She drew in a deep breath. "You're right. I like you. I was just scared to admit it."

Ty took her hand. "And now?"

That was the ultimate question, wasn't it? "Now, I'm still scared, but I don't care anymore." A lie detector went off inside her gut. She cared plenty; she was just trying harder to push those cares aside. "I know it can't last, but maybe that's okay. Maybe it doesn't have to last to be worth it."

Ty drew his eyes together. "Why can't it last?"

But he must've known why. "My life is in Chicago. And your life is here." It was the easy answer, and the only one she could give right now.

"What if—"

But Camille cut him off. "Let's have dinner Friday night."

He blinked. "Instead of Bug Fest on Saturday?"

"In addition to it."

He grinned. "So, your plan is to spend as much time together as possible?"

She hesitated. "More like, enjoy the time we have while it's here."

Ty's smile faltered. "I can live with that. For now."

Chapter Eleven

The next day, a set of hands grabbed Camille from behind and hustled her into the main barn. Nikki folded her arms, tapped her foot and tilted her head to the side. It was classic Nikki. *I'm your younger sister and I'm not letting you off the hook.* "I just talked to Dillon. What gives?"

What were Camille's chances of getting out of this if she played dumb? "I don't know what you mean." But she knew it hadn't worked before the last word was out of her mouth.

Nikki's fingers extended and folded over as she counted things off. "A, you know exactly what I mean. B, we're running out of time. And C, what are you thinking?"

Nope. No way out of this.

Nikki stepped closer, staring her down. "Dillon said Ty doesn't know anything about the offer on the house. Are you gonna tell him?"

"You told Dillon?"

"Just answer the question."

"I'll tell him."

"When?"

"Today?" It would have been more convincing if it hadn't come out sounding like a question. Camille cleared her throat and tried again. *"Today."*

Blue eyes drew suspiciously together. "You still want to sell, right?"

"Of course I do."

"So why are you stalling?"

"I'm not."

"You had all day yesterday."

But Camille didn't have a good answer for that because she wasn't really sure herself. She and Ty hadn't had one fight yesterday. And Evie was smiling again. And she didn't want to ruin any of it. So why not just tell Nikki that?

Because you think Ty is a fling and don't want Nikki convincing you otherwise.

No, no. Fling was all wrong. A summer romance, maybe. And a brief one at that. He couldn't possibly be more, not when he lived in Nebraska *and* flew planes *and* had no intention of giving up either. But her inner voice was right that she didn't want to get into all of that with Nikki.

"Is Dillon gonna tell him?" She didn't want Ty hearing it from anyone but her.

Nikki sighed. "No. He's giving you the chance to say something first. So?"

She had one passable excuse for delaying things that Nikki couldn't argue with. "Ty said he wouldn't sign any sales papers until after Phoebe's wedding. That's still nine days away. There's no point bringing it up now."

But Nikki had an answer for everything today. "The way Ty makes googly eyes at you, he'll sign the papers this afternoon if you just ask him." Camille bit her bottom lip, and Nikki's voice softened. "Look, if you're having second thoughts—"

"I'm not. Our home is in Chicago. That's where we belong."

"Okay, then go tell him."

"He's not on the ranch right now. He had to run into town."

"So, tell him when he gets back."

"I won't see him until dinner."

"Then tell him at dinner."

"With Evie right there? She might get upset. She really likes Ty."

Nikki rubbed her temples. "Look, the buyers who made the offer love the house and think Ty's whole airstrip thing is kitschy or something, but they won't wait forever. Neither will the bank back home."

Check and mate. "Okay, fine. I'll tell him tonight."

"Pinky promise?"

Oh, no. The calling card of doubting sisters everywhere. Camille's mind raced for an excuse. Was there such a thing as a sprained pinky finger? "I, um…"

Nikki was holding her pinky up and ready, inching it closer. The barn door opened and Evie ran in. Emmitt came in just behind her. Camille's hand balled protectively around her pinky and flew down to her side. "Evie wants ice cream," Emmitt said. "But I told her she had to ask first."

Camille nodded. "Sure, her aunt Nikki can get some for her."

Nikki put her pinky down and shook her head, but Evie's smile was still so new it could win over the iciest of aunts. Evie grinned, and Nikki walked her out of the barn and toward the house. The second Nikki was gone, Camille dug her phone out of her pocket. Ty had plugged his Wi-Fi password in days ago so she could use it when she was here, but it didn't work in the barn.

She peeked outside. Josh was walking toward the stables, Dillon and Daisy were over by the hangar and Ty was still in town. Coast clear. She stepped out of the barn and dialed Ben's number.

"Attorney King's office."

"Hi, it's Camille Bellamy."

"Oh, Camille, he's in court right now. You

want his voice mail or you want me to take a message the old-fashioned way?"

"Voice mail's fine, thanks."

It chimed over and Camille fumbled through her message.

"Hey, Ben, it's Camille. Listen, I just wanted to double check something. What would the bank say if we were a few days late getting the money to them? We've got an offer on the house, but it might take a little longer than I'd hoped to get it all signed. Just let me know, thanks."

She hung up and stood there a minute, wondering why she had even made that phone call.

Options. You want options, that's all.

Right, it was always good to know your options. No one could argue with that, not even Nikki, who was walking toward her across the yard. She must've pushed ice-cream duty on Emmitt. Camille hurried in the other direction, before Nikki's pinky could come out and grab her.

Ty needed tonight to be perfect, and so far everything was going wrong. He got to Camille's twenty minutes early, then thought maybe that was *too* early. So he cut his engine and sat in her driveway. Except someone must've spotted him pull up, because five minutes in Camille opened the door and asked if he was just gonna sit there.

Strike one.

When Ty parked his truck on the curb at six o'clock in what accounted for downtown Sweetheart, the line for the newest pizza parlor hot spot, You Wanna Pizza Me, was just starting to slide out the door. *Great.* An hour earlier and there'd have been no wait at all. Strike two.

He opened the door for Camille and Evie, and they hopped out. But when he shut the door, he shut it on the hem of Camille's light blue skirt. It came out unharmed, and she laughed it off, so he was calling that a foul ball instead of strike three.

But there was still the hostess issue. She gave him the bad news, and he returned to Camille, afraid their game might be over. "Twenty minutes for a table."

Her expression didn't change, which didn't help him a whole lot. His experience with kids and restaurant wait times was zero. He pictured hungry tantrums and dirty looks from other customers. "We can go somewhere else if you want."

His mind tried to come up with something suitable for vegetarians, and he got another big fat zero. *Focus.* All right, there was an Italian place down the street and a sub sandwich shop a little farther down from there. Not the most romantic spot, but good for kids and vegetarians. Thankfully Camille saved his brain from having to work any harder than it already was.

"Twenty minutes isn't bad. Besides, you said

something about a game room?" She cracked a smile and dimples the size of Texas shot out the corners of her mouth. Evie's eyes glowed, and Delaware dimples shot up at her corners. Another couple of years, and they'd probably give Camille's a run for her money.

He took a buzzer from the hostess and showed them into the game room, where a Skee-Ball game was ready and waiting. He fished a few dollars from his wallet and got Evie some quarters. Turned out she was a Skee-Ball whiz. While she was playing, Camille nudged his arm.

"I need to talk to you about something."

Ty's stomach tightened. She'd changed her mind again, hadn't she? They only had a week left, and she didn't see the point in date-night pizza or tomorrow's Bug Fest. It was back to being friends. Only Ty wasn't so sure he could handle that anymore. Not after the last kiss they'd shared.

Visions of Mia cropped up, invading Ty's head with negative thoughts he didn't need. Mia was over. Done. A part of his past. Camille was here. Now. Right in front of him. He touched her arm, just to make sure she was real, and smiled when his fingers confirmed what his mind already knew.

"What's up?" He meant for his voice to sound casual, but it came out tight.

She bit her bottom lip. "It's just that…um…" And just when he was sure she was about to give him bad news, she changed direction. "The Foosball table's free, and I've never been beaten."

Ty laughed, relieved. "Never?"

"Nope."

Challenge issued, challenge answered. They set things up, and Evie beat them both. He was about to declare a best-three-out-of-five challenge when their buzzer went off and the waitress led them to a corner booth.

"You were right," Camille said after they'd ordered a large thin crust with tomatoes and peppers. "This is fun. Thanks for taking us here." Her voice sounded bright and there was a smile on her face, but her eyes didn't match either one of them. And when she folded her hands on the table, her wedding ring laughed at him.

"I'm glad you're having fun," he said, wondering if she would ever take that ring off and hating himself for thinking like that. It wasn't that she'd been married before; it was the constant reminder that in a lot of ways she still was. And Ty had no idea how to fix it.

She sipped her soda and shot Evie a look. "There's a jukebox in the corner. Why don't you put something on?" She gave Evie some quarters, and Evie went to make her selections. Camille turned back to Ty. "So, how would you feel about coming to visit us in Chicago sometime?"

Visit? Chicago? "Cities and me don't exactly get along." The words were out of his mouth before he'd had a chance to check them.

She nodded. "That's what I thought."

Don't blow this.

All right, if Chicago wasn't in his future, that meant Sweetheart had to be in hers. "I know you think Chicago is home, but I've got a whole week to prove you wrong. And if we don't get an offer on the house soon, maybe even longer."

She picked up her straw wrapper and started rolling it into a ball. "Ty, there's something I've got to—"

"Oh, hi!" Avery's voice cut off Camille's.

The ball Camille had been rolling dropped. "Hi."

Avery and Smith were walking toward them, hand in hand. Either Avery didn't notice the stilted way Camille was talking, or she was just in too good a mood to care. "You'll never believe it. I called Emmitt today, and we talked for almost a half hour. He's coming to the wedding."

Smith put his arm around Avery's waist and kissed her cheek. "I told her not to give up. Her brother's stubborn, but he's smart enough to know he's only got one sister."

Camille's mouth dropped open. "You're Emmitt's sister? His *engaged* sister?" Her startled cry was loud enough to turn heads even in the busy restaurant.

Ty looked at her. "I told you that."

"No, you most certainly did *not* tell me that."

Huh. Ty thought it over. Maybe she was right. *Wait a second.* The relief at finding out who Avery was…the glaring looks she'd been giving her… Had Camille been jealous?

Camille walked around the table to give Avery a hug. "Congratulations. When's the wedding?"

"A few weeks."

"And Emmitt wasn't planning to go?" Camille frowned.

Avery delivered the perfect bittersweet smile. "Emmitt and I had kind of a falling out a couple years ago, but Ty's been helping me patching things up, and I think they're finally turning around."

Evie came back over. Avery said a quick hello, then ran off with Smith before someone stole their table. Camille was smiling now, and this time the smile went straight to her eyes. What had they been talking about before? "You had something to tell me?"

Camille shrugged. "Only that I'm happy to be here."

"I'm happy too." He took her hand and gave it a squeeze. Tonight had started out shaky, but it had really turned around. Now if only he could figure out a way to make Camille stay in Nebraska.

Hey, God, I know I've been difficult, but if You could help me figure this thing out, I'd sure appreciate it.

God didn't answer, but Ty rejected the anxiety that crept up his spine at the Big Guy's silence. God answered things in His own time. Ty got that now. Until then, Ty would try to fix this on his own.

Nikki was awake when Camille and Evie got home. It was just after nine o'clock. "So how was it?" She got up from the couch.

"Fun. Not the same as a Chicago deep dish, but still good."

Nikki looked at Camille expectantly. "And…?"

Camille ran a hand through Evie's hair, combing out a tangle. "And… Evie beat me and Ty at Foosball. Twice."

Nikki sighed and looked at Evie. "Is it time for pajamas?" Evie yawned and went upstairs without making a fuss. Camille tried to follow her, but Nikki grabbed her elbow. "Hang on a second."

Was Nikki really gonna demand details two seconds after she walked through the door? She could already hear the millions of questions about to come her way. Was there hand-holding? Cuddling? A good-night kiss? Yes, no and best kiss ever.

When Evie went to put more quarters in the jukebox, Ty had leaned over and kissed her. It was quick, and it only happened once, but all the warmth she saw in his eyes had spread through his lips and warmed her toes.

Instead of asking questions though, Nikki walked over to the answering machine and hit play.

"Camille, it's Ben. I tried your cell but you're probably out of range again. I double-checked with the bank like you asked, and as long as you've got proof of an impending sale, they'll hold off on the foreclosure. But that means they need to see signed papers by the thirtieth. No wiggle room there. Call me back tomorrow if you've got questions."

The machine clicked off and Nikki turned to her, arms folded, face scrunched. Camille knew that look well. *Explanation?*

Sigh and double sigh. What was she supposed to say here? "I just wanted to know what our options were, so I called Ben."

"Thanks for filling me in." Her voice sounded a little hurt.

"I'm sorry. I only wanted to…" What? Find excuses to leave Sweetheart? Find excuses to stay? "To weigh things out."

Nikki's arms were glued across her body. "Did you talk to Ty?" It was a yes or no question.

"Define talk…"

Nikki's breath came out in one long groan. "Okay, fine. Maybe it's better that we stay here. Evie loves it, and I'm a little tired of city life anyway. Who says I can't sell houses in Nebraska just as well as Chicago? I'll just call the buyers tomorrow and tell them the deal's off."

"No." Camille jumped forward, almost tackling Nikki to the ground. "Don't do that. Don't do anything."

The strained look on Nikki's face said it all. *You're acting ridiculous.* Camille couldn't argue with that.

"We might not have a choice," Nikki said. "You got a call from Ben, but I got a call from the agent the offer came through. They wanted to know what the holdup is."

"What did you tell them?"

"That we were weighing our options. That's vague agent talk for we might have another offer."

"Do we?"

"No, but I didn't want to lie, and I didn't want to tell them the truth, so vague was the best I could come up with. Their agent thought I was fishing for more money, and he told me flat out there's another house the buyers are interested in. They want an answer by 9:00 a.m. Monday or they're withdrawing the offer."

"Monday?"

"Yep."

Okay, she could work with Monday. That was days away. A whole weekend. Both Saturday *and* Sunday. She'd chickened out of telling Ty about the offer tonight, but that was hardly her fault. Not when Avery had dropped that double bombshell. Emmitt's sister? Engaged? She felt silly for ever being jealous.

Not jealous.

Just…protective. She'd felt protective of Ty. Now that she knew she didn't need to feel so jeal—protective—she'd tell him about the offer tomorrow. For sure this time. Definitely. Probably.

Chapter Twelve

Camille ran around shoving things into her bag for Bug Fest and pleading with her sunglasses to show themselves. Her sunglasses ignored her entreaties, probably whispering behind her back about the basket case she had become over the last few weeks. All thanks to Ty.

Best. Kiss. Ever.

The thought came out of nowhere, and her smile lasted maybe two seconds before it flickered out and she stood frozen with her hand on the sunblock.

Best kiss ever? She used to think that about her first kiss with Wesley. A horn beeped from outside and Nikki's voice called up the stairs. "Ty's here."

Things started snapping into place again, but she felt like she was moving in slow motion. She added the sunblock to her bag along with an extra change of clothes for Evie, just in case any of the bugs left a trail of slime running up her arm.

The front door opened and Ty's voice floated into the house. Camille's feet stuck on the top landing. What would Wesley say if he were here?

What a silly question. If Wesley were here, she'd never have kissed Ty. If Wesley were here, she wouldn't be going to look at bugs. If Wesley were here…

But Wesley wasn't here. He'd been gone two years, so why did caring for Ty feel like a betrayal?

She'd promised Nikki not long ago that she'd ask God for His help sorting this all out. She had two days to tell Ty about the offer or let it slide by. Two days to decide her future. Now seemed like a good time to give God a try.

God, if You're listening, can You give me a hand? Please? I need some sort of sign that Ty and I are supposed to be together.

Maybe that wasn't fair, laying her entire relationship with Ty on God's shoulders, but wasn't that what He was there for? To help people through their burdens?

Was Ty a burden now? She didn't mean it like that. She had to stop thinking this way. Her relationship with Ty had nothing to do with her relationship with Wesley. They were completely different. Except they weren't. Wesley and Ty both flew planes, had both fought for their country, had both crashed. The only difference was that Ty had survived.

The stairs creaked and Camille jumped as Nikki's face came toward her. "Are you coming?"

"Yeah." Camille smiled brightly, but Nikki narrowed her eyes.

"Are you okay?"

"Sure, just excited for some bugs. By the way, if any come home with us, you're in charge of getting rid of them." She raced down the stairs.

Nikki raced after her. "I didn't agree to that."

Downstairs, Ty was picking Evie up and flipping her upside down. Camille's first impulse was to cringe, but Evie's giggles quickly pushed her anxiety aside. Kids Evie's age were supposed to do things like that. Tumbling and climbing trees—all things that made parents nervous but which kids somehow managed to survive.

Ty smiled at her. She returned it, but inside her stomach started to spin. Evie looked so much like Wesley it was almost like having him in the room. Ty set Evie gently down and moved in to kiss Camille. She turned her head and took a step back, then felt guilty for it.

A flicker of doubt blinked in Ty's eyes, and then it was gone. He shifted tactics, giving her a half hug instead of the kiss he'd intended. Nikki gave her an odd look and mouthed something to her behind Ty's back. *What's wrong with you?*

Good question. Camille wished she had a good answer.

"All right, let's go see some bugs." Camille tried to make her voice cheery, but it was hard to get excited about things she normally squished and threw down the toilet.

Ty looked at Nikki. "Dillon asked me to tell you his lesson today got bumped to nine instead of eight, so he was hoping you could make lunch an hour later."

"Thanks, I'll text him." Nikki whipped her phone out and started typing.

Camille's throat felt dry. She'd forgotten about Dillon's flying lesson. It would be great for the ranch if business picked back up, but more lessons meant more flying, and more flying made it impossible to ignore the fact that Ty was a pilot.

Nikki grabbed her as they were going out the door and whispered in her ear. "Tell Ty about the offer. Don't forget." As if she could forget.

Outside Bug Fest, the parking lot was crammed with cars. Ty hadn't lied when he'd said this thing was popular. They found a spot in the back and walked to the nature center. There were trees and flowers and trails everywhere, kind of a mini arboretum.

Off to the left Ty pointed out a stream, and just

past it, if you squinted real hard, you could make out Sky High Ranch. A little farther beyond it and a lot more squinting, and you could almost see Sweet Dreams.

"I didn't even know this place was here." Camille took Evie's hand. Ty took hers. She almost pulled away, but stopped herself. She liked the way his hand felt around hers and had no reason to feel guilty about it.

Glass tanks with bugs from all over the world lined every path and walkway. They started outside the center and wrapped their way inside and out the back. Evie stared at a tarantula who was busy crawling up its owner's arm. Camille had seen a movie about killer spiders once and was fairly certain the tarantula's goal was to eat the man's head.

When he offered to let Evie hold it, Camille almost had a heart attack. But Evie immediately held her hand out for it. The man set the tarantula in Evie's palm and it began to crawl. Camille squealed and covered her eyes. When she dared a peek, Ty was snapping a picture.

"Don't worry, you don't have to look. You can see the pictures later."

She nodded and closed her eyes again until Ty tugged on her arm. They were moving down the line. Evie had just spotted something called the Goliath beetle. It was the size of a small apple and just as shiny. She waited in line for her chance to pet it.

Ty came over. "You okay? You look a little green."

"Maybe I just need some water." She reached into her bag and brought out a bottle.

"Do you have another one? I didn't think to bring any." His stomach rumbled, and he blushed. "Guess I'm hungry too. I sort of rushed breakfast this morning."

She pulled out a bottle of water and some snacks. "I've got blueberry muffins."

"Like the ones you made for the gift basket?" He was staring at them.

"I froze a bunch and defrosted them last night." He didn't immediately reach for one, and by the look on his face he wasn't sure he wanted to. "You liked them, didn't you?"

He stood frozen a moment, then broke into a grin. "Sure I did. Thanks." He took the muffin and started chowing down.

If she was gonna tell him about the offer on the house, now was the time. His mouth was full, so he couldn't argue with her. And they were surrounded by people. She was pretty sure Ty wasn't the sort of guy who liked to make scenes.

So, how to start? "Nikki got some news the other day."

Ty finished the last bite of muffin. The tiniest

crumbs were stuck to the corners of his mouth. She brushed them away and felt his breath on her fingertips. It made her toes tingle, and when she looked in his eyes, the world stopped.

He swallowed his muffin. "What about Nikki?"

"Huh?"

"You said Nikki got some news?"

"Oh, yeah." Her mind had completely blanked in the time it took to look in his eyes. "She… um…she loves Phoebe Saylor and is dying for her autograph. So, we've got to keep an eye on Nikki next Saturday and make sure she doesn't corner Phoebe during the wedding."

It wasn't a lie. Nikki really did love Phoebe Saylor, and Camille wouldn't put it past her sister to follow Phoebe down the wedding aisle till she got her autograph. As for the offer on the house? She still had tomorrow. Maybe she'd let today slide.

Over by Beetle Row, Evie smiled and waved as she moved from the Goliath beetle to some jeweled beetles that would have been pretty if they weren't still bugs.

In the distance the steady hum of a plane began to sound. Camille looked up and recognized one of Ty's planes coming across the sky. Dillon's lesson must have started. Evie looked up from the bugs and waved as if Dillon could see her all the way from up in the clouds.

The plane dipped down, zigzagged a little, then did a slow turn. It was kind of fun, their own private airshow. Except that thick black smoke started trailing out behind the plane, a lot like Buffy when she was in serious trouble. And the steady hum of the engine turned into an erratic chug.

"What's wrong?" Camille asked.

Ty frowned. "I don't know."

The weird noise it was making got worse. It was louder now, more like a deadly cough. The plane turned back toward the ranch, moving away from them. She had to squint to make it out, and then the black smoke turned to orange flames and squinting was no longer necessary. The plane nosedived toward the ground, and for half a second everything stopped, then chaos broke out.

Don't panic. Stay calm. Keep focused. Ty repeated the mantra over and over again in his head as he raced back to the ranch. He tried Dillon's cell and got no answer. He tried the house phone and got nothing there too. If anything had happened to Dillon, Ty would never forgive himself. *Just find him fast.*

Camille was in the passenger seat. Ty kept looking at her, expecting her to freak out. But she looked calm. *Too* calm. It was one of her brave fronts. She was better at putting them up than he'd realized.

Evie was the only one crying, and she was doing it silently. Somehow that made it worse. Just when he was getting used to her newfound fits of giggles, she gave him this. What did he do with it? How did he help her?

"Dillon's a good pilot. A *great* pilot. I'm sure he's okay." Ty didn't know whether he was trying to convince them or himself. The black smoke rising up in the air left a lot of room for doubt.

When he pulled up to the ranch, Daisy ran toward him. "Josh and Maricela took the Silverado. He was pretty close when he went down."

That was good. The faster they got to him, the better. "Who else was with him?"

"No one."

"What about his lesson?"

"They canceled last minute. Dillon took the plane out anyway. Said he wanted to test it out after the last repair."

Camille had one arm around Evie, trying to comfort her. Daisy was waiting for orders. Four years in the army was a hard habit to break. She wanted something to do, and Ty was the one in charge here.

"Daisy, stay with Evie and Camille. Call the fire department and get some trucks down here. I'll go after Josh and Maricela."

He had the engine running and his foot on the gas when the Silverado's squeal caught his ear. He looked up and saw the red truck speeding toward them. Maricela was driving. Josh was in the passenger seat. The back was empty.

They couldn't find him.

Ice pricked his veins and turned his body cold. They needed a plan. That was always step one. Everyone could spread out. Ty would take his truck; Josh and Maricela could go back out in the Silverado. There were other trucks and plenty of horses. He'd get everyone together and—

Josh's prosthetic hand was hanging out the door waving Ty over. There wasn't time to talk. The situation required action. But mindless action was as bad as doing nothing at all. There was an order to these things. *Talk, plan, act.* He ran to Josh.

Camille watched him, her face showing every crinkle of concern. "Did you find the plane?" Ty asked. It was important to know whether Dillon had gotten up and walked away or if he might still be trapped inside.

"We found it." Josh turned his head toward the back seat, and Dillon's head popped up. He'd been lying down; Ty had just missed him.

Every muscle and nerve in Ty's body relaxed. Until Ty took a closer look. Black ash was smeared across Dillon's face. His clothes were stained and his head was bleeding, but it was his leg that worried Ty the most. It was twisted at an odd angle.

"He was trying to walk home when we found him," Josh said.

Dill grinned, but his face was pale under the ash. "I figured if I couldn't walk, I could always hop."

If Dillon could make jokes, that meant it couldn't be too bad. Unless there were internal injuries. Jon's battered face flashed in front of him, replacing Dillon's for a second. Panic tried to surf in on a tidal wave, but Ty pushed it back. It was getting easier to stop, especially knowing Camille and Evie were watching.

"Okay, Maricela, you're already in the driver's seat. Get him to the hospital. Josh, stay with her. I'll follow in my truck."

Maricela took off, and Ty hurried back to Camille. "Is he okay?"

"I think his leg's broken. I'm heading to the hospital."

Camille was already moving for the truck. "We'll go with you."

He shot a look to Evie, whose tears had slowed but were still coming. "You sure about that?"

"Evie will feel better if she knows he's okay. Me too."

There wasn't time to argue with her, and the

truth was being near them helped. If he could, he'd always keep them within an arm's reach. They jumped in the truck and got to the hospital a few minutes after Maricela, who must've been an amateur race car driver at the speeds she'd been going. Dillon was already with the doctors.

This was the worst part. Time to wait. Ty had never been great at waiting. New plan—keep his head clear and everyone calm. Vending machines were a good place to start. He fed a few dollars into the machine and stocked up on chips and candy. Evie helped pass them out to a growing crowd in the waiting room.

Everyone from Sky High was at the hospital now. Nikki showed up looking pale. She'd seen the plane go down and called over to the ranch. Daisy had filled her in. She and Camille conversed quietly together in the corner.

Emmitt was in the opposite corner sitting with his knees curled to his chest. Evie went over and put one arm around his neck before taking the seat next to him. Nikki left Camille and went to talk to Maricela. Ty took her place at Camille's side.

"You okay?" he asked.

She nodded. "You?"

He shrugged, reaching for her hand. She let him take it, but she didn't squeeze back. Her fingers just lay there dead against his own. He let her go, and she curled her hand into a fist before shifting uncomfortably on her feet.

Ty knew she was upset. The dimples were down for the count, and he doubted he'd be seeing them anytime soon.

"Dillon's gonna be fine," he said, wanting it to be true. Maybe if he said it enough times, it would be.

Camille was staring at her feet. "I wish I was as brave as you."

Ty tried squeezing her hand again. "You are." This time she pulled her hand away.

"No, Ty. I don't think so. I don't think I'll ever be."

But Camille wasn't giving herself enough credit. She was stronger than she realized. How did he make her see that?

Daisy tapped him on the shoulder. "I think Emmitt's losing it."

He looked at the corner of the room where Emmitt was leaning over in his seat, his head buried in his hands. He looked ready to start climbing the walls. Camille nodded in Emmitt's direction. "Go on, he needs you."

Ty let out a breath. "I'll be right back." He hurried over to Emmitt's side, replacing Evie's now-vacant chair.

Emmitt could barely look at him. "It's my fault." His voice was a croak.

"What's your fault?"

"Dillon. It's my fault he went down. I checked Cessna 1 this morning. Whatever went wrong… I missed it."

There was no way he was gonna let Emmitt carry this on his shoulders. "And I checked the Cessnas myself two days ago. And what about the repair guy who was just out here? Everything looked good then too. This is no one's fault. Sometimes things just go wrong." But Emmitt kept his eyes on the ground.

The doctor came out. A couple dozen people crowded in around him. Ty held his breath, waiting for the prognosis. "Dillon's going to be fine. No internal injuries."

A joint sigh filled the waiting room. Several people clapped the doctor on the back. It was the best possible scenario under the worst possible circumstances. Dill's leg was broken in two places, but they were clean breaks. His face and body were bruised, his ego was probably shattered, but all of it would heal.

Ty turned to get Emmitt's reaction, but he was gone. When he turned back around, Camille was standing there. "Nikki's gonna hang around. Think you can give her a ride home? She drove Buffy down here, and I'm gonna drive her back. I want to get Evie home."

"Sure." He hesitated. "Are we okay?"

She pressed her lips together. "Why don't you stop by tomorrow after breakfast? We can talk then."

Talk? The universal breakup code. Maybe he was overreacting, misreading her stress for something that it wasn't. "Aren't you coming by Sky High tomorrow? I thought we were gonna finish up in the house."

The foot shuffle started, and she spun her ring around her finger at least a dozen times. "Maybe later in the day. I think tomorrow we'll sleep in. Come by around nine, unless you're here."

"Sure. Want me to call you later?"

"No, thanks. Nikki can fill me in. I think Evie and I need some rest. It was kind of a long day."

It wasn't even noon yet, but he knew what she meant. He started forward, wanting to give her a hug. She didn't pull away, but hesitation flickered across her face. It made him pull back. "If you need anything, let me know."

She smiled, but it was bittersweet. "Same here."

When she walked out the door, it reminded Ty too much of Mia walking out the door. He almost ran after her, desperate to fix this before Camille left for good. But the doctor was letting people in to see Dillon, and Ty was up first. Everything else would have to wait.

Chapter Thirteen

~❦~

Breakfast was too quiet without Dillon there. Josh tried to fill in the gaps, making jokes and telling funny Dillon stories, but it wasn't the same. After a few minutes Josh's jokes fizzled out and things got quiet again.

Too much quiet equaled too much time to think. Ty had spent the night trying to convince himself he'd misread Camille's signals. Things yesterday had gotten out of control. She was upset. It would make sense if he'd confused her shock waves for breakup blips.

And even if he hadn't, so what? Things could easily have changed overnight. If they hadn't, he would find a way to make them change. Camille wasn't Mia. And there was no way he was letting her out of his life now that she was in it.

He headed to Sweet Dreams as sprinkles started falling. The rain was supposed to last all day and carry through the week, until Saturday, when God had decided to break tradition and do Ty a solid. The rain would give way to blue skies and sunshine. Just in time for Phoebe's wedding to go off without a hitch.

Ty rang the bell to Sweet Dreams, trusting that everything would be all right once the door opened and Camille invited him inside. But when it opened, Camille stepped out and clicked the door shut behind her.

"Hi." He looked for anything that might tell him what she was thinking, but the signs were as vacant as her eyes. The only thing he saw was a manila folder in her hand.

"Let's walk." Camille started for a path that looped around her property. No hello. No good morning. Just her head down and her eyes on the ground, like this was a chore she couldn't get out of. "How's Dillon?"

Finally some sign the Camille he cared so much for was still in there. That this was maybe, just maybe, all in his head.

"Doing okay. The doctor said he could come home Wednesday. They just want to make sure nothing unexpected springs up."

"Nikki will be happy to hear that. She was ready to pack a bag and spend the night at the hospital."

The sprinkles turned to a light mist that felt good on his face. "If I tell Dill that, it'll only make his ego worse. He already thinks he's likable, now he'll know it."

Camille didn't even crack a smile. Another bad sign. Should Ty break the silence or let it linger? Maybe she was thinking about all the good things in their relationship. That wasn't the sort of thing he wanted to interrupt.

But the way her lips were turning down made him think if he was in her thoughts at all, they weren't good ones. "I thought we could try fishing next week instead of bugs."

That got a reaction from her. She finally looked at him. "I don't think so."

What was he thinking? "Right, vegetarians probably don't fish. Forget that. Ever been on a boat? We've got a canoe in the storage shed. I can pull it out and buff it up. It'll be fun."

"Ty—"

"I know what you're gonna say, but it's perfectly safe. I'm a great swimmer, and I've got plenty of life vests."

"Ty, stop. Don't say that."

He replayed his last few words, not sure where he'd gone wrong. "Say what?"

Her brow crinkled. "Don't tell me it's safe. That's what you always say. About the horses, about the planes, and none of it's true. None of it's safe. I should never have let you convince me it was."

Careful or you'll make things worse. "Camille, I know those things seem scary, but there's danger in everything we do. You could get into an accident driving a car, or swallow your food the wrong way and choke. At some point, you have to stop worrying or you'll never be able to enjoy the life you have."

It sounded like something out of a made-for-TV movie, but it was true. And he could see in her eyes she knew it.

"We got an offer on the house."

The ground fell out from under him. "What?" His voice came out in a croak.

"A few days ago. I meant to tell you sooner, but we were having so much fun." She tapped the manila folder in her hand. "Nikki's got the paperwork together. I just need you to sign it."

It was even worse than he'd thought, and it made him angry. "What about Evie? Is this fair to her? Running every time you're scared?"

Her blue eyes turned red. "I'm doing this *for* Evie. And we're not running, we're going home. There's a difference."

They had stopped walking and were facing each other. Camille's hands were on her hips, and her eyes dared him to keep arguing with her. This time he wouldn't back down. He knew what she was doing and why she was doing it, even if she didn't. And he wasn't about to let her get away that easily.

"I love you." He didn't rush the words; he said them loud and without embarrassment.

Her cheeks burned pink and she started walking again. Fast.

"Camille, stop." She almost tripped over her own feet, but she stopped moving. Her back was to him.

"I love you, and I know you love me too even if you're too scared to say it. So I'm gonna do us both a favor and tell you now that I'm not signing those papers."

He waited for her reaction. When she turned around, she was crying. "But you've got to sign them."

"No, I don't."

"You promised."

Her bottom lip trembled, and Ty felt caught. He *had* promised. Breaking his word to Camille was just him being selfish.

"I said I'd sign them after the wedding, and I will. If that's what you really want, but not until then." It would buy him a few more days at least. Give him time to think his way out of this.

Her tears turned to anger. "You still don't understand. It doesn't matter if I care about you, I can never be with you. Not in a week, not in a month, not *ever*."

The back of his neck was burning. "Why not?"

The crescendo was building inside her. He saw it rising up behind her eyes, and it burst out of her like a volcano. "Because you're a pilot."

Camille's words crushed Ty's heart, and they weren't done.

"I can't let myself fall in love with you, Ty, because I can't put myself through that again. I won't do it. I refuse to."

She tipped her head back defiantly. Ty went to her anyway. For one moment she allowed him to hold her, and then she pushed him away.

"Please, don't. It'll just make things harder. I'll always be grateful for what you've done for Evie, but it's easier this way. It's better. For me and Evie both." She shoved the manila folder into his hands, then turned and ran away. Conversation over.

Camille buried her head in her pillow. All she wanted to do was crawl under her blankets and pull the covers over her head like she used to when she was a little girl frightened by a thunderstorm. Only she wasn't a little girl anymore, and this was no thunderstorm.

She'd thought telling Ty goodbye would be easy. Well, maybe not easy, but easier than this. Right now her chest ached and her stomach was swimming backstrokes. It felt almost as bad as when she'd learned Wesley had died—*almost*. But it would all be worth it if it meant Evie was safe. And she'd be safer back in Chicago, away from wild horses and crashing airplanes.

And if anything ever did happen to Ty, she wouldn't have to hear about it. She could live on in blissful ignorance. There was a time when she thought truth was all that mattered. Now she knew better. Ignorance was far safer for your emotions than the truth would ever be.

A soft knock sounded on her door. Camille dried her face with her bedsheets. "Camille?" It was Nikki.

Not now. Camille wasn't up for whatever kind of talk it was Nikki wanted to have. But Nikki wasn't going away. She knocked again. Camille stayed silent.

"Okay, but if you don't answer, I'm gonna have to assume something terrible's happened to you. Like you were hanging a picture when a mouse crept into the room and cornered you. And now it won't leave until you provide it with cheese. Do you need some cheese?"

Camille sat up in bed and curled her knees to her chest. A smile formed on her lips. She tried to fight it back and lost.

"Or maybe a lion escaped from the zoo and is holding you hostage with its massive paws. I have pepper spray in my room. Cough once if you want me to get the pepper spray."

Camille giggled and the door pushed open. Nikki blinked and looked around the room. "I thought I heard you cough, but I don't see any lions."

"Does Sweetheart even have a zoo?"

Nikki shrugged and sat on the edge of her bed. "Tell me what happened. I'm guessing Ty wasn't too happy."

"It's my own fault. I never should have kissed him. I never should have done a lot of things."

"You like him. That's not something to be ashamed of."

She wished it were that easy. "This isn't about Ty. It's about what's best for Evie. Whatever's between me and Ty is just… It's no big deal." Something slapped the back of her head and she winced. It was Nikki's hand. "Ouch. What was that for?"

Nikki's eyes drew together. "How many men have you kissed since Wesley?"

Camille stared at her hands. "None. Well, one. Ty."

"Exactly. And that's why this thing with Ty *is* a big deal."

Maybe. But it didn't matter. "We're leaving Nebraska as soon as the wedding is over."

"Ty hasn't signed the papers yet."

"He will. He's mad right now but he won't go back on his word. He said he'd sign them after the wedding, and he will. He's just hoping I change my mind before then, but I won't."

Nikki leaned back on the bed. "You're sure?"

"Positive."

"I guess that means I've got to work my people skills and get the buyers to hang on a few more days."

Camille arched her eyebrow. "Do you think you can?"

"Maybe. But it couldn't hurt to say a prayer."

Evie came into the room and pointed to her stomach. Time for a snack.

"I'll make you something," Camille said. "Go downstairs and I'll be right there." Evie smiled and bounced happily away.

Nikki threw an accusing glance at Camille. "You haven't told Evie yet, have you?"

No, she hadn't. What difference did it make? "Evie knows Sweetheart isn't permanent."

"But she's six, and she's gotten pretty attached to some of the things and people around here, don't you think?"

"And when we get back to Chicago, she'll get reattached to the things and people there."

There was another sigh coming. Nikki shook her head. "You know I'll always love and support you, whatever your decisions are, but are you sure this is really what's right for Evie?"

Why did everyone keep asking her that? "Yes, I am."

Nikki didn't look convinced. "When's the wedding?" Again with the questions.

"Saturday."

"And when do you want to leave?"

Camille screwed her face up. "Sunday. Maybe Monday."

"That's less than a week and you haven't told Evie yet? I thought you were doing this for her."

Camille stood up. "I am."

Nikki stood up too. "All right, then tell her. See what she thinks about it."

It was a challenge, but it was one Camille would win. Evie had to miss their home in Chicago just as much as she did.

Downstairs, Evie was already at the table. Camille went into the fridge for carrots, hesitated and pulled out ice cream instead. It wasn't a bribe—it was just covering her nutritional bases. Ice cream was part of the dairy food group.

Evie's eyes lit up, and Camille gave her an extra scoop. She set the bowl in front of her and took a seat as Evie dug in. "Honey, there's something I want to talk to you about." Evie looked up, and Camille felt the air grow suddenly hot. She pulled at the collar of her shirt.

"It's about Ty. No, no, it's about this ranch." That was better. Kind of. Evie's brow started to scrunch. "It's just that we got this really terrific offer on the place, so we're selling it and going home. Next week. Isn't that great?"

Evie dropped her spoon and pushed her bowl away unfinished. She held her arms out at her sides. *What?*

"I know you like it here, but there's more for you to do in the city. Don't you miss it there?"

Evie shook her head. Camille bit her bottom lip and reminded herself that kids didn't always know what was best for them.

"Once we're back, you'll be happy. You'll see."

Evie got up and went over to a side table where several of her drawings were piled high. She searched through them all and grabbed one of Ty in front of an airplane. She pointed to him and lifted her shoulders.

"No, Ty's not going with us."

Evie glared at her and kept pointing to Ty.

"Honey, I'm sorry. He can't come with us. He wouldn't want to anyway. His home is here." But that was the wrong thing to say. Evie threw her drawing on the floor and ran away from the table. "Evie, wait." Camille followed her upstairs, but Evie had already shut and locked her door.

Nikki stood in the hall. "I guess Evie doesn't think moving back is what's best for her after all."

Camille rounded on her sister. "That's because she's six, Nikki. I'm her mother, I know what's best and it's in Chicago. So please, if you really meant what you said about respecting my decisions, then back me up on this. Otherwise just don't say anything at all."

Camille went back downstairs and outside to the porch. Nikki, wisely, did not follow.

Chapter Fourteen

Hump day was extra lumpy this week, and Ty was ready for it to be over. He walked into the house and went past Camille without saying a word. She was sitting on the living room floor with her legs crossed. Wooden signs were spread out around her, and she was hand-painting directions on all of them.

Reception, right arrow. Bathrooms, left arrow. Ceremony, straight ahead. Evie was off with Daisy and Maricela, and Dillon was supposed to be coming home in another hour or two. Ty was just waiting for the official call to go pick him up from the hospital.

The hammer Ty wanted was on the counter where he'd left it. He grabbed it and went past Camille again on his way to the door. One of her signs tripped him, and he almost fell on his face. She didn't even look up, just moved the sign closer to her so no one else could trip on it.

Ty turned for the door. Camille's iciness was giving him frostbite, and it was just a little too much for him this early in the morning It wasn't even ten o'clock yet. He opened the door and almost ran into Maricela.

"Where's Emmitt?" Her words cut through the silence, an alarm bell that jangled his nerves.

"I thought he was at the stables."

Emmitt had skipped breakfast this morning, but that wasn't totally unusual for him, especially when he was on stable duty. He'd rather get out early and take the horses for a ride than sit around and eat bacon.

Maricela shook her head. "He's not there. I just checked. No one's seen him all morning. And the horses are all in their stalls." Ty's anxiety began to creep.

Camille was looking up now. "Maybe he slept in."

But even as she said it, Ty didn't really believe it. Emmitt woke up before the birds. He went to Emmitt's room and knocked. No answer. He tried again. Still nothing. Ty wasn't the type of person to invade someone's privacy, but he had to know if there was a problem.

"Emmitt? I'm coming in." He pushed the door open and poked his head into an empty room. Ty shut the door and went back downstairs. Camille and Maricela both looked at him. "He's not there."

Maricela's shoulders sagged.

"Let's not overreact," Ty said. "Emmitt likes his walks. He's probably just out on one of the trails. Why don't we give it a couple hours before we start worrying? Emmitt deserves our trust." It was what Dillon would say.

So why did he feel like he should be sending out the cavalry? Trust shouldn't be so hard. Neither should love. He glanced at Camille, who was back to ignoring him completely, then went outside and headed for the barn. He kept his eyes open for Emmitt's dark-haired figure bobbing amongst the prairie grass.

A few of the horseshoes Camille had decorated for the dairy barn were on the ground. He hung them back up, then said hello to Milkshake. Evie had paid her a visit earlier today, but Milkshake didn't mind the extra attention from Ty.

He started sweeping hay and double-checked that more of Camille's decorations weren't about to fall. It was all busy work, designed to keep him away from Camille. Knowing she was inside the house but totally unapproachable was driving him nuts.

The scar on his arm started itching. It hadn't itched like this in a while, but all week long it had been bothering him. He pulled the sleeve of his shirt up and scratched it like a mosquito bite. The itch turned to a burn, and the warmth began to spread.

It's all in your head.

Yeah, yeah. He knew. It had burned plenty after his plane went down and Ty emerged as the solo survivor, but since then it only sparked up when he was under stress. He scratched it harder.

"Stop. Just relax." Talking out loud to a room full of cows couldn't be a good sign. Ty was losing it.

No. Not losing it, losing *her*. Losing *them*. And there was nothing he could do about it.

It's a test.

That had to be it. God's final joke. It was unfortunate, because Ty was about to fail. He looked up at the roof, seeing beyond it toward an invisible creator who passed His time playing games with people's hearts.

"I give up. I'll never beat You. Whatever I do, You do better. Whatever I get, You take away. So guess what? You win. And we're through. Too bad. Just when I was starting to like You again."

A throat cleared behind him, and Ty turned to find Dillon standing there, a crutch propped under each arm and his leg in a cast. "Do you and your invisible friend need a moment alone together? I could come back later."

Ty broke into a grin and drew Dillon into a careful hug. "When did you get back?"

"Just now. Josh got me."

"I thought you were gonna call."

"I did. You didn't pick up. So I tried Emmitt. He didn't pick up either. Josh is the only one who likes me well enough to answer."

Ty looked at his phone and saw three missed calls. "I must've been spacing out. Sorry." He stared at the phone. The last call was from an hour ago. "Emmitt didn't answer?"

"No. Why?"

"He hasn't been around this morning. He wasn't at breakfast either."

Dillon frowned and pulled the keys from his pocket. "I'll take the Silverado. You saddle up Honey. We'll find him in no time."

But Ty grabbed the keys from Dill's hand and stuffed them in his pocket. "You're not going anywhere. Especially not now. It's supposed to start storming in a couple hours and you're down one leg."

"Yeah, but it's not my driving leg."

Ty kept his head straight on his neck, folded his arms across his chest and spread his legs hip-width apart. It was a power stance. He'd learned it watching his superiors in the navy. Effective for two things—getting an extra dessert at meal-time and making people squirm.

"You shouldn't be out here. Let's get you settled in. I'm sure Emmitt's fine." *Probably* fine. As soon as Dillon was sitting down, he'd get Maricela and the others and put Dillon's scouring idea into practice. He started for the house. Dillon stayed where he was.

"So, is it God you are giving up on or just yourself?"

A groan rose from Ty's throat. He was hoping Dillon hadn't heard all that. God was really playing him for a fool today. "You need to rest your leg."

"I'll rest it when you answer my question. Is it you or God?"

Man, he was stubborn. A lot like Camille, actually. "Both." He pulled a Camille and arched one eyebrow, daring Dillon to say something about it, but his arch didn't have the same effect. Dill kept going.

"You can't just give up on God. I know my crash shook you up, but it was God who got me through it. He's the reason I'm alive right now."

This was already too drawn out. Ty wanted it over and done with. "I'm not upset because of the crash. I mean I am, but…"

"It's Camille." There was no getting anything past Dillon. "Nikki said you guys haven't talked in two days."

Three, but who was counting?

"If you want Camille to stay, then go fight for her. Tell her you love her."

"I already did."

The bottom half of Dillon's jaw dropped open. "You did?" Ty nodded. "And?"

"And she said she can never love a pilot. Not after what happened to her first husband." That ought to end this discussion.

Now it was time for Dillon's know-it-all younger-brother look, perfected when Dillon was a mere six years old. "So, don't be a pilot then."

Ty's brain melted a little bit. "What?"

"If it's that important to her, and you love her, then what choice do you have?" He hobbled a little closer. "Didn't the idea of giving it up even occur to you?"

No. It hadn't. And for good reason. The thought of never flying again scared him. No, *scare* was way too small a word. It terrified him. And he was talking a towering inferno kind of terror. "Flying's all I know."

Dillon wasn't gonna let him off that easy though. "It's not *all* you know. It's one part of you. There are a lot of other parts too. Camille's one of them now. Maybe it's time to focus on that."

Ty's head was hurting. "But the ranch won't make it if we stop flying."

Dill shifted on his crutches. "I didn't say *we* should stop flying. I said *you* should."

But how would that work? "Even if I did, she won't stay. She's going back to Chicago."

"So? Go with her."

But Dillon was asking the impossible. His voice was hoarse when he spoke again. "I can't. What if something happened and I wasn't here?"

Dill sighed. "Whatever you're scared of, is it scarier than losing Camille?"

The question was simple, but it hit him in a big way. Every dark cloud hanging over Ty's head vanished, and every doubt he had vanished with it.

Nothing was scarier than losing Camille.

Ty tucked the sales papers Camille had given him into the manila envelope and went to find her. She wasn't in the house. He finally spotted her by the stables against a gray backdrop of clouds. The air was misty but warm, and she was pulling up folding chairs as fast as she could.

She'd set them up earlier today to make sure they wouldn't topple over during the ceremony, but with the rain coming, she had to get them put away or they might blow away. She must not have heard him coming, because she jumped when she saw him. A big jump too. She backflipped over one of the chairs and landed on her face.

Ty hurried to help her up. She took his hand, then immediately shook it off. "I'm fine."

"Sorry if I scared you."

"You didn't." She turned away from him and went back to her chairs.

"You haven't seen Emmitt, have you?" *Stop stalling.*

She kept her back to him. "No. Is he still missing?"

"Yeah, I'm starting to worry."

"Should we go look for him?"

"Dillon's getting some of the guys together."

"That's good."

It was great she was talking to him, but her short clipped tones didn't exactly ease his anxiety. She turned toward him, and the wind whipped her hair across her face. He stepped closer and pushed it out of her eyes, tilting her chin back so she was looking at him. For one moment it felt like better times, then she stepped back and nearly collided with the chairs once more.

"Ty, you need to leave. Please. I can't go through this with you again." She started toward the house.

He started after her. "Camille, wait." But she only walked faster. "Wait." Another minute and she'd be sprinting. "I won't fly anymore."

Camille stopped. Slowly she turned to face him. "What?"

It was now or never. "I'll stop flying. I'll give it up. As of right now."

A silent film played out in front of him. Her lips were moving, but no sound came out. Her expressions were overdrawn, her eyes about to pop. "But…but you love flying."

"I love you more." He didn't even have to think about it.

Her eyes started spinning out of control. "What about the ranch? Won't you lose it?"

"No. Dillon will keep the lessons going. Emmitt and Maricela can help him. They both have training."

"So you'll be here, you just won't fly?"

"No, I won't be here at all."

Her eyes widened and her mouth started moving again before her voice came out. "You…you don't mean Chicago."

He nodded. "You asked me once if I'd come visit you there. What if it wasn't just a visit?" Her face paled. "I don't mean move in with you. I'll get my own place. We can take things as slow as you want, but at least we'll be in the same state."

Ty wasn't entirely sure what he'd expected, but it certainly wasn't the greenish look on Camille's face right now. "Ty…" He took her hand, but she pulled it back. "Ty, no. I can't let you do that."

He didn't get it. "You're not making me do anything. I want to do this. I love you, and I need you." Even more than he'd thought he needed Mia. His love for Camille surpassed everything else. *Everyone* else.

But her face moved from green to stark white. She shook her head. And he finally understood. This was one thing he couldn't fix.

"It's not planes you're really scared of, is it? It's me." She took another step away from him, and his body felt numb. Why hadn't he seen this before? It could've saved him a lot of heartache. "Planes are just an excuse. It's love that really scares you. And nothing's gonna change that, is it?"

She didn't contradict him. She just started twisting her wedding ring around. Ty stared at it, and after a moment she looked down and saw what she was doing. She hadn't even been aware of it.

Now it was Ty who took a step back. "I love you, but you know what? I deserve someone who can love me back. And if that's not you…then maybe you're right. Maybe this can't work." He handed her the manila envelope.

"What's this?"

"The paperwork. I signed it. Go ahead, sell the house. Keep whatever you get for it too. I don't want any of it."

"George wanted you to have—"

"It doesn't matter. George was a great man,

but he's not here anymore. And I won't have my life ruled by the past. George wouldn't want that for me either."

Every muscle in Ty's body wanted him to stay where he was, but he forced himself to turn around.

"Ty, wait." He paused, one last flicker of hope. "I'm sorry."

The last flicker went out. "Me too."

Camille found Evie and Nikki feeding the goats. No one else was around. Camille pulled Nikki aside. "I'm going into town. Can you stay with Evie?"

"Sure. Everything okay?"

Was it? "Ty signed the papers." She held up the envelope.

Nikki paused, a handful of oats in her palm. "I thought he wouldn't sign until after the wedding."

She didn't want to get into the details of what had just happened. "He changed his mind. I'm gonna fax them to Ben before he changes it again. We'll be back in Chicago by next week. Just like I planned."

Evie was staring at her now. She ran up to Camille and wrapped her arms around her waist, shaking her head from side to side. Camille kneeled down and gave Evie a hug. "Sweetie,

Chicago's our home. You've probably missed it and don't even realize it."

But Evie didn't seem to share that opinion. Her eyes darted to the manila envelope in Camille's hand, and she tried to grab it. Camille pulled it out of reach and stood up, staring down at her daughter. Overhead, distant thunder cracked, the perfect backdrop for Evie's tears.

Nikki rested one hand on Evie's shoulder. "I'll get Evie home before the rain starts. You go on." Both of them stood together; neither of them looked happy. But Camille didn't have a choice.

She called Ben on the way into town and could almost hear the smile in his voice when she told him the papers were signed. The signal lasted a full two minutes before cutting out, just long enough for him to congratulate her.

There was a fax machine in the copy center where she'd printed all of Phoebe's pictures. A friendly clerk greeted her. "What a day, huh? I heard they spotted a tornado in the next county." *Tornado?* She'd better get this done fast.

She double-checked the paperwork to make sure Ty hadn't missed anything, then realized she hadn't actually signed it herself. She grabbed a pen off one of the tables, but when she went to sign, her hand started shaking.

What's the matter? This was what you wanted. Of course it was. *Is.* She drew in a deep breath and pressed the tip of the pen to the signature line, but when she willed her hand to move, it just sat there. All she could think about was Evie's smile, and the way Ty had said he'd loved her. Her heart had gone kerplop in those few minutes.

A crash of thunder overhead punctuated her frown, and the sprinkles that had been threatening to turn to rain finally kept their word. She looked out the window and saw Emmitt walk past the splotch-covered glass. He was holding a brown paper bag.

Oh, no. She shoved the papers back into the envelope and hurried after him, careful not to move too fast or get too close. He hadn't seen her, and the last thing she wanted to do was send him running.

Her phone was at the bottom of her purse. She dug it out and saw a missed call from Nikki. She dismissed it and dialed Ty without even thinking twice. He answered on the first ring.

"Ty? Don't hang up."

"Why are you whispering?"

"I found Emmitt. He just crossed the street from Banana Blitz."

His voice was strained. "Stay with him. Don't let him see you. I was already headed into town. I'll be there as soon as I can."

Emmitt turned, and Camille ducked behind a parked car. She peeked through the rain-splattered windows and saw him head toward a liquor store. Her breath froze mid-inhale, but he walked right past it.

Relief washed over her until he turned a corner and fell out of sight. She sprinted to the end of the block and spotted him pulling out an umbrella, waiting to cross the street. Camille wished she'd thought to bring hers.

She hung back and watched him cross over to the park. The bench was empty. He sat down and dug into the paper bag.

No, Emmitt. You don't have to do this.

Her phone buzzed, but she ignored the incoming text from Nikki and watched Emmitt. Maybe she should stop him. She could take away his bottle just as easily as Ty.

One foot started moving in his direction, but it stopped when he pulled out a loaf of bread. He tore off tiny pieces and tossed them to an eager flock of birds who crowded in around him. When Ty pulled up, Emmitt was still feeding the birds.

Camille hesitated, not sure what to do, then crossed the street and joined them. She was already wet, she might as well get soaked. Ty was trying to get Emmitt in the truck. "Do you know how worried we've been? Why'd you take off like that?"

Emmitt continued feeding the birds. "You don't need me."

Ty sat down next to him. "That's not true. You're important to everyone on the ranch."

"Dillon almost died because of me."

Ty stopped him with an emphatic shake of his head. "The crash wasn't your fault."

"How do you know?"

Camille put one hand on Ty's shoulder. "Ty and I saw Dillon's plane before it went down. Black smoke was coming out of it."

"That's right. Dillon said the exhaust system was leaking gas and caught the engine on fire. That's a defect with the exhaust system. If anything, the repair guy missed something when he worked on the fuselage, and that's not your fault. It might not even be the repair guy's fault. Sometimes things just happen."

Emmitt looked up. "Is that true? That's really what happened?"

"Ask Dillon yourself. He's home right now."

Emmitt looked down at the bread in his hands. "I'm such a fool."

"Well, if you're a fool here, you can be a fool at home too. Let's go."

Emmitt started laughing. One of Ty's lopsided grins emerged, and Emmitt started for the truck.

Ty pulled Camille aside. "Thanks for your help."

She felt her cheeks color. Why was it so hard to say goodbye? Maybe because part of her didn't really want to. Ty's eyes fell on the wet manila envelope she was still holding. "Did you send the papers to your lawyer? Already?"

She hesitated. "You signed them. I thought we were done with this."

He moved away from her. "I guess we are."

Emmitt was already in the truck, watching them.

Her heart was beating too fast. "I'm sorry if I hurt you, Ty. I want you to be happy."

He shook his head. "It's not about my happiness. It's about being true to yourself and facing your fears with God's help."

For one second the impulse to kiss him was almost too much. Everything Ty did and said made her love him all the more. Which was precisely why she had to leave this place.

Wait. Did you just say love?

She told her inner voice to hush up. Now wasn't the time.

Emmitt interrupted them, "Are you coming, or should I head back without you?"

"I'm coming," Ty said and headed for the truck.

Camille's phone buzzed again, and this time she looked down at Nikki's text. Evie's gone! Get home now.

The clerk's tornado warning flashed back to her. Ty's engine roared to life. Camille ran toward it before he could take off. "Ty, wait!" His door opened, and he stepped out of the truck. She grabbed both his arms. "Nikki just texted me. Evie's missing."

Inside the truck Emmitt must have heard her, because he sat straight up and looked at her through the window.

"Get in the truck," Ty said.

"But Buffy."

"You can get her later. I can get us there faster."

She couldn't argue with that. Emmitt scooted to the back as she hopped in the front. Ty put the truck in gear and took off almost as fast as the lightning that flashed in front of them.

Chapter Fifteen

It felt like they were crawling at a fast twenty as Ty moved them down the dirt path back to Sky High. Ty shut off the radio. Camille was just barely holding it together without tornado warnings every five minutes.

Emmitt was doing a good job of keeping her calm, talking about anything and everything that popped into his head. Ty was focused on getting them back fast and safe and only heard bits and pieces of the conversation.

"...and then I dropped my ice cream down Avery's shirt... Co-Coe could eat her weight in bacon... Evie's gonna be all right..."

Camille was doing a lot of nodding. Every time thunder cracked, she jumped in her seat. When the ranch finally came into view, Camille swung the door open while the truck was still rolling.

For one second his heart did a high jump waiting to see if she'd fall and be crushed. She was fine, but Ty was gonna have to talk to her about jumping out of moving vehicles. For someone who was scared of everything, she sure knew how to push the boundaries of danger.

The rain was really coming down now, but at least they still had some light. It peeked out behind the gray clouds and lit up the land just enough to see people spread out, dressed in rain-coats and calling Evie's name.

Nikki was talking to Dillon and Maricela under the porch cover. Her eyes were red. She turned to Camille and her face crumpled. "I'm so sorry. I took her home and thought she was in her room, but when I went to check on her, she was gone. I thought maybe she came here, but…"

Camille hugged her sister tight. "It's not your fault. We'll find her." But when she turned back around, Ty saw the look in her eyes. That brave front had been for Nikki's benefit. Camille was terrified.

Okay. Time to move.

He already knew the plan. He'd spent the drive back putting it together, starting with Dillon. If he didn't give his brother something to do, Dill would figure out something to do on his own and end up hurting his leg all over again. Step one: get his little brother out of the way. Step two: make sure they weren't missing the obvious.

"Dillon, you and Maricela take the Silverado.

Go back to Sweet Dreams with Nikki. Look *everywhere*. She might still be there."

Nikki shook her head. "I checked all over."

The last thing Ty wanted to do was be rude when Nikki was already upset, but he had to be sure. "In every closet? Behind every tree? In the crawl space?"

"There's a crawl space?" Nikki's eyes drew together. "You're right. We need to check again. I've got my phone."

She hopped in the truck with Dillon, and Maricela sped off.

Daisy was the next closest to him, and she was standing by awaiting orders. "Did anyone take the horses?" Ty asked.

"Not yet."

"Okay, I know it's rough out here right now, but we need someone on horseback. We already know Evie moves fast when she wants to."

Emmitt stepped forward. "I'll go. I'm good with a horse. Honey's scared of snakes but couldn't care less about thunder."

Ty wasn't sure sending Emmitt out alone into the storm was a good idea given all that had happened, but he really was the best with a horse.

All right, God. I'm trusting You to help us out on this one.

"Okay, Emmitt. Thanks."

"I'll go too," said Daisy. "I can ride Pepper.

We'll cover more ground if we split up." Pepper was the only other horse Ty trusted not to get spooked in this kind of weather.

He nodded. "Take walkies."

Whatever worries were swimming around Emmitt's gray eyes, he kept them to himself. He turned to Camille. "Evie's strong. She'll be fine." Then he was gone.

"What about me?" Camille asked. "What should I do?"

Desperation had crept into her eyes somewhere between town and the ranch. Her hair was plastered to her head, making the desperation more obvious. And desperate people acted without thinking. That was never good for anyone.

"You and I are gonna start at the dairy barn and work our way out. Evie's got a thing for animals, right?" Camille nodded. "We need to check every loft, every haystack, every—"

"I've got it. I'll meet you there." Lightning couldn't have moved faster. That was good. It meant she was moving with purpose. He told everyone else to spread out, stay in pairs and take a walkie if they headed out of cell range. Ty grabbed a walkie for himself and went to join Camille.

This was the part Ty hated most. The one where hope and doubt brawled it out inside him. He *hoped* he'd walk into the barn and find Evie tucked safely in Camille's arms. Her hair would probably be covered in hay and she'd give him one of her cute-kid smiles and everything would be okay again.

But it was doubt who met him at the door. Inside the barn Camille was the only one with hay in her hair, and there was no Evie in her arms. Her eyes were spilling out a never-ending waterfall, and she was spinning in a slow circle. "Evie!"

The only response came from Milkshake. Even if Evie heard them, she wouldn't answer. Calling out to her was only making their voices hoarse, and it was getting them nowhere fast.

He climbed the ladder to the loft and peeked over the edge. There was no one up there. A thin layer of hay covered the floor, not nearly enough for anyone to hide under. Not even a little girl. He climbed back down and almost tripped on Camille. She was hovering at the bottom rung, staring at him.

"Why didn't you go up?" she asked.

"I just did."

"But you didn't go *up*. You just looked around. That's not the same thing. You said to check everywhere."

"Camille, she's—"

But Camille was already moving past him, climbing the ladder and crawling into the loft herself. He didn't try to stop her. Heavy foot-steps sounded above him as she stomped from one end of the floor to the other. They stopped, and he expected to see her feet appear over the edge. When they didn't, he got nervous.

"Camille?" He climbed up the ladder after her. She was on the floor with her knees curled to her chest.

"This is my fault." A sickly rattle was at the back of her throat, muffling her words. "I told Evie we were moving back to Chicago, and she didn't want to go."

Ty sat down next to her and put his arm around her, gently stroking her hair. They were covered in shadows, but there was enough light to see that her skin had turned pale. "You were just doing what you thought was best for her."

A choked sob-laugh broke free from her chest. "That's just it. I wasn't. Not really. I kept trying to tell myself I was doing what was best for Evie, but I wasn't even close."

She pulled back and looked at him. The bright blue of her eyes mixed with the gray shadows and cast a strange dark glow across her face. A stray strand of hair fell across her forehead. Ty pushed it out of the way and Camille held her breath.

"Ty, everything you said was true. I was scared of my feelings for you. And I did the most un-forgiveable thing any mother can do. I used Evie as an excuse to get away from you." A tear ran down her cheek. She let it run. "If I've lost her, I'll never forgive myself."

Ty squeezed her hand; she squeezed it back. "Evie's gonna be okay. I promise." Camille would be okay too if she could just get out of her own head for a minute. "You don't have to forgive yourself. That's God's job. All you have to do is trust in Him, and He'll get you through this."

She blinked back more tears. "I'll try. I really will."

All right. Enough. Ty stood up. He took Camille's hand and helped her to her feet. "Come on."

"Where are we going?"

"The hangar. Evie likes the planes almost as much as she likes the animals. She could be hiding in one of them."

Camille's eyes widened. "That's a good idea."

They hurried to the hangar, but it turned up just as empty as the barn. Camille didn't crumble though; she steeled her gaze and kept looking. And Ty got an idea. He pulled up the Doppler radar and checked the crosswinds. Fifteen knots. Ty had flown in worse, and the Cessna could handle twenty. Thirty if he pushed it hard.

The tornado was hovering in the next county. If it moved over, he might get into trouble, but until then he could manage things. He grabbed the keys for Cessna 2 and opened the other half of the hangar door.

When the first plan doesn't work, make a new one.

"What are you doing?" Camille asked.

"Going up. We've already got people on horse and on foot. Plan B is the Cessna. I'll take her up and see what I can find."

Alarm sounded in Camille's eyes. "Is that safe? Dillon's plane crashed and it wasn't even raining."

"It's safe enough. The Cessna's stronger than the Piper in a storm like this, and I'll cover way more ground in the air." He got into the pilot's seat and realized his heart was beating hard. The last time he'd flown in a storm was the night Jon died. "Go look in the house. Who knows, maybe Evie—"

"I'm going with you."

Ty blinked, positive he'd misheard her. "What?"

She was moving toward the plane. "I'm going with you. How do I get in?" She tried to hop up and almost fell on her behind.

This wasn't the time for her to put on a brave front. Ty hopped down and helped her off the ground. "Camille, it's not gonna help if you go up there and panic. It's better you stay here."

"I can't stay here. I'll go nuts if I do."

Now was the time she chose to face her fears? "It's too dangerous."

"You're not scared." But part of Ty *was* scared. Part of him was terrified.

"You're staying here."

"I said I'm going." She had her hands on her hips. That mama bear look was coming out again. This was no front—she was serious.

"If something goes wrong…"

It was at least two deep breaths before she answered. "You said it was safe. I trust you…and I trust God."

Ty couldn't believe he was about to say this. "All right then, let's get you in the air."

Don't look. Whatever happens. Just. Don't. Look.

"You okay?" Ty was seated beside her. That was good. She needed him close right now. But when he turned the key and the engine roared up, that was all she could hear.

Oh, dear God, please, oh, please, oh, please, don't let us die.

She drew in a deep breath and let it out. *Trust.* She trusted God, and she trusted Ty. She'd just have to remind herself of that over and over and over again. Probably for the entire time they were in the air. And how long would that be exactly?

But that was an easy one to answer. She would stay up there until she found her daughter. That one thought was enough to calm her. Finding

Evie was all that mattered now. And with Ty and God both on her side, she could do this.

She opened one eye and saw Ty staring at her. "Ready?" he asked.

"Let's go."

He radioed something to the others, letting them know what was going on, then he took them out of the hangar and down the runway. The plane shuddered, and she let out a squeal. Ty looked at her. That had to be the last place he should be looking. "I'm fine, I'm fine. Eyes on the road."

She closed her eyes again. Better she didn't know what was going on until it was all over. She would just keep her eyes closed the entire time. That was all. Ty could tell her when they were safe on the ground again.

Ahem. Captain? We have a problem.

Right. If she kept her eyes closed the whole time, she wouldn't be able to look for Evie. Why did her inner voice choose this moment to start making sense?

Okay. Fine. She would open her eyes, but only because she owed it to her daughter. If there was even a chance of finding her from a thousand feet up, she had to take it. Wait. A thousand feet? Was that even right? What if it was more?

She opened one eye and tugged on Ty's shoulder. "One second." He pulled back on the controller. It looked like a big stick coming out of the floor. The front of the plane tipped back, and the nose went up into the air, fighting against the rain. Thunder sounded, and Camille swallowed the scream rising on her lips.

The plane was coming off the ground. It peeled off the grassy runway and there was actual air beneath them now. Ty turned back to her. "What's up?" Her mouth forgot how to move, and her voice couldn't speak. "Camille, are you okay? You want me to take you back?"

He started moving like he meant to bring the plane back down. She found her voice. It was weak, but it was there. "No. Keep going."

There was his lopsided grin. His warmth spread to her even as they cut through the air, and she reached out one hand to touch his shoulder. As long as she kept it there, she felt safe. Ty was her rock, or in this case, her wings.

She knew he was only a man, but oh, my, if he didn't fly like an eagle. The ground kept falling away from them, but the plane felt steady even in this wind. She had no idea how he was doing that. The plane leveled out, and instead of her heart exploding, it found a new rhythm. A steadier rhythm than what she was used to even on the ground.

A low flying cloud looked close enough for

her to touch, and something inside her she didn't even know had been off flipped on.

Oh, wow. I get it.

Being in the air was like being one step closer to Heaven.

"Let me know if you see her," Ty said.

It was easier looking at the clouds than at the ground, but she had to do it. For Evie. For Ty. For herself. She squeezed Ty's shoulder and moved her eyes down. The first glance was a downward spiral. She had to shut her eyes fast or she was afraid she'd fall out. Everything was upside down, and her heart was back to skipping beats.

But it didn't last. Ty's hand came off the control wheel, just for a second, just long enough to squeeze hers. It was all she needed. Had she really tried to convince herself she didn't love him?

One more time.

She opened her eyes, and the land below them came into sharp focus. A few deep breaths and she got through the initial shock of it.

"How high up are we?"

"About a thousand feet."

She forgot the clouds and kept her eyes on the ground. Evie was down there somewhere. The only light they had was gray and dismal, but they were close enough to the ground that it was enough. Anything bigger than a mailbox came into focus.

On their left, Honey was racing down a dirt path. Emmitt's shadowy figure was easy to pick out even from this high up. On their right, Daisy was riding Pepper as fast as she dared.

Ty turned the plane. It was a gentle curve, not a roller coaster. The wings tipped to the left and the ground began to shift under them. Something caught her eye farther north of them.

"There." She pointed toward a large tree with pink blossoms growing out of it.

Ty veered the plane in that direction. "I'm gonna bring her in a little closer."

The plane dipped down, and any panic Camille might've felt at the sudden change in height was overshadowed by the possible sighting of Evie. They cut their distance in half, and Evie's face lifted toward them from over by the tree. Her hair and clothes were plastered to her body.

"Evie!" Camille waved to her daughter.

Ty looked at her. "Camille, stay in your seat. Don't get up."

Was he kidding? She wasn't gonna jump out from this height, no matter how happy she was to see her daughter. Evie looked up at them and her mouth dropped open. Slowly she lifted one hand and waved back.

"Stay right there. Don't move."

"Camille, she can't hear you."

But she didn't care. She kept waving, and Evie

kept waving back. "How do we land this?" She searched the ground for a spot for Ty to set down.

He chuckled. "We don't. Not here anyway."

"But Evie."

"I'll radio it in. We passed Emmitt back there. Give him a minute to get over here. We'll keep circling till then."

Evie was standing now. She started jumping up and down and jogging along with the plane trying to keep up.

Camille's eyes teared up. When Emmitt finally got there, Evie was nothing but a great wet blur. But she was safe. And as long as Camille had that, it didn't matter if Evie ever talked again. Talking was overrated anyway.

The plane touched down and Camille expected to see Evie running toward her, arms outstretched, but she didn't even see Emmitt. She started getting up and Ty's hand immediately shot out and pushed her back into the seat.

"Not yet. The plane's still moving." He sounded serious. Maybe she ought to listen. Her mind was just moving so fast, and her feet were anxious to catch up to it.

She tapped her foot, then switched to making fists with her hands. How long did it take for a plane to come to a complete stop anyway? And where was Evie?

No matter which direction she looked in, all she saw was open space, puddles and a whole lot of *not Evie*.

Finally Ty let her go. He took her hand to help her down, and she felt his pulse beating beneath his skin. A steady rhythm that jumped ever so slightly at her touch. He put his other hand on her waist so she wouldn't fall, and their noses bumped against each other.

A horn started honking, breaking the moment they were inching toward. She turned and saw Maricela barreling across the runway toward them in the Silverado. Dillon jumped out too fast and his crutches slipped in the mud. One fell over, and Nikki picked it up for him. Her blond hair spun in a circle as her head did a three-sixty scan. The rain was letting up a little now. "Where's Evie?"

Good question. She turned to Ty. "Where are they? Do you think something happened? Should we go back for them?"

He took her hand and squeezed it. "Deep breaths. Evie's fine. Emmitt was on a horse. We were in a plane. It's gonna take him a little longer to catch up, that's all."

But Camille wouldn't really believe Evie was okay until she was here in her arms. She found north and started walking that way, wanting to meet them.

Nikki and Ty followed after her. People kept congratulating her as if she'd done something special. It was Ty who'd found Evie, with God's help. All Camille had done was sit in the plane and...

Sit. In. The plane.

Oh. She'd just flown in an *airplane*. So much had been happening all at once, the magnitude of that hadn't really hit her until just now. She stopped walking and looked at her sister.

"What?" Nikki wiped rain out of her face.

"I flew in a plane."

Nikki blinked. "This isn't a good time for jokes."

She shook her head. "No, really. I went up with Ty looking for Evie."

Nikki looked at Ty, seeking confirmation. The smile on his face was enough for her. Nikki's jaw dropped open.

"You know what else?" Camille said. "I didn't die. Nothing bad happened. In fact, just the opposite."

"Don't tell me you liked it." Nikki was shaking her head now, disbelief firmly planted in her eyes.

Camille shrugged. "I kind of...did." It was hard admitting that, but she wasn't gonna hide her real feelings anymore. Not from herself, not from others.

Ty's grin went wild. He didn't even have to say anything, all he had to do was look at her and she knew he was proud.

"There she is," Nikki said, pointing.

Emmitt's horse came into view. Evie was sitting in front of him, grinning. For half a second, the horse stopped and Emmitt's figure was silhouetted against a darkened sky with streaks of sunlight shooting out from behind the clouds. A real-life cowboy, and Evie's new hero.

He hurried toward them, and the second Evie was within grabbing distance, Camille reached for her. She cradled her daughter in her arms, shedding happy tears for once instead of the exhaustive supply of sad ones the last two years had afforded.

No more tears after today. Only happy times from now on. It would be a new rule in their house, along with pizza parties every Friday night.

When she finally let Evie pull back enough to breathe, there were tears running down her cheeks too. They blended with the sprinkles still coming down.

Camille kissed her head. "Evie, I know you were mad at me, but you can never run away like that again, okay? Do you know how scared I was? How scared your aunt Nikki and Ty were?"

She hugged Evie again, not wanting to let go.

A tiny squeaky sound came out of the mass of wet golden hair. "I…"

Camille froze. "Did you…did you say something?" Around her, Ty, Nikki and the entire ranch stopped the chatting that was going on and looked over.

Evie's bottom lip pushed out. Her eyes colored with flecks of gold, and she drew in a breath. "I… want…to stay…here."

Camille started trembling. Ty was at her side in an instant. Was she really hearing this? She looked at him for confirmation and found it in his eyes.

It was Camille's turn now. "You want to stay here in Nebraska?" Evie nodded. "With me and Aunt Nikki?"

Evie drew in another breath. Her lips parted. "And… Ty." Evie looked at him, and Camille's heart quickened. There were tears in his eyes. Love was drawn in every line of his face, for her and Evie both.

She kissed the top of Evie's head. "Of course we can stay. This is our home. We belong here." For the first time in two years, she wasn't scared. God had just given her everything she'd ever asked for. Now it was up to her what she did with it.

Chapter Sixteen

Camille stared at her reflection in the mirror. She was wearing a light blue dress Nikki had surprised her with, and her hair was down around her shoulders in soft waves. She would have looked great if she weren't so pale. Her heart was running sprints inside her chest, and she didn't think it was gonna slow down anytime soon. Not until she got this over with.

The wedding ring she'd worn on her finger for the last six years shone brightly back at her, winking. Camille touched it gently, afraid it knew what she was about to do and might bite if she tried to follow through with it. She'd just have to let it bite.

Slowly she began twisting it around her finger. And then she began twisting it *up* her finger. She stopped before it came off, already feeling the empty space where it used to sit and cringing. Then she drew in a deep breath and pulled it off.

The ring burned in her palm as she squeezed her fingers over it. "I'll always love you, Wesley, but I've got to let you go now." Tears ruined her mascara. She looked around for a safe place to store her ring and thought of George's purple heart still in the nightstand.

She opened the drawer, kissing the ring before setting it in the case. George's Bible lay beside it, unopened. The binding was worn and inside the pages were probably creased, but that was only because George had used it so often. Those creases were his love for God.

Camille took the Bible out and opened it. An envelope fell to the floor from between its pages. She bent over to pick it up, and her already light head got that much lighter. Printed in George's squiggly handwriting was her name.

For just one second she hesitated, then she ripped it open. Inside was a single page folded over. Camille unfolded it and laughed at George's first words.

Camille,

I love you like a daughter, but you're the most stubborn person I know. Then again, it takes a hardhead to know a hardhead.

I don't want you to sell the house right away. It's for your own good. You've been running from things for too long, only I was too chicken to tell you so when I was alive. Now that I'm gone, you've got no choice but to hear me out.

Ty's a good man. I think you'll like him, and I respect what he does. I care about him almost as much as I do you, so I'm leaving him the land. At the very least, he'll slow you down if you try to sell. At the very most, you two might be friends. I think you could use a few of those.

Don't be mad at me. I'll tell God and Wesley hi for you when I see them. Now go be happy.

Love always,
George

It was dated just before he'd left to go to the hospital, where he'd finished out his final days. Camille drew in a breath and wiped her eyes. She put the letter back in George's Bible and left it sitting on top of the nightstand instead of locked inside it.

It took fifteen minutes to fix her makeup, and when she got to Ty's, she was running ten minutes behind. It was a good thing Nikki had taken Evie over early. She'd claimed it was for Evie's benefit—more time to pet the horses. But Camille suspected it had something to do with cute kids being more likely to get autographs from movie stars. And Phoebe wasn't the only celebrity here. Of the hundreds of guests, half were faces she recognized.

A bazillion photographers and reporters inundated Sky High, snapping pictures of everything and everyone. When they asked who the event designer was, one of the bridesmaids pointed out Camille. They took her picture and asked for the correct spelling of her name. Camille tried to keep her cool, but it was difficult with flashes going off in her face.

A strong hand took hold of her arm. "Excuse me," said Ty, "Ms. Bellamy is badly needed in the barn. It's a decorating emergency."

The photographers gave her a path of escape, and Camille took it. "What's the emergency?"

"You looked like a deer in headlights. I wanted to make sure you got out of the way before you were struck down."

"Thanks." She smiled as Nikki and Evie walked over.

"Phoebe wants to see you," said Nikki.

Evie tugged on Nikki's sleeve and held up a sheet of paper. "Don't forget this." Talking was still new for Evie, but one or two words a day was more than Camille had gotten in the last two years. She'd happily take it.

Nikki's cheeks flushed as she took the paper.

Phoebe Saylor's autograph was sprawled across it. "Thanks." She slipped it in her pocket. Camille told Ty she'd meet up with him later and went to check in with Phoebe.

"I just wanted to thank you for everything. I don't know how you pulled off so much so fast, but it's perfect." She was wearing a knee-length wedding gown like something out of a 1950s magazine. Beautiful, fun and it wouldn't get all muddy. The ground was still damp in places.

The ceremony went off without a hitch, even when Pepper decided it would be fun to walk backward with the groom when he was trying to put the ring on Phoebe's finger. Everyone laughed, including Phoebe, and when Pepper brought him back over to finish up, they all applauded.

They'd gone with a live band, and it turned out the hangar could pretty much double as a concert hall. The acoustics were great. Ty asked Camille to dance, and she took his hand as they made their way onto the makeshift dance floor.

He spun her around and pulled her back to him, and when her hand touched his arm, his lopsided grin faded away. Ty stared at the empty space where her ring used to be, then shifted his eyes slowly to hers. A question lurked behind them.

Camille shrugged. "It was time."

She knew most of Ty's looks, so his kiss came as no surprise. Warmth swallowed her up and her heart started keeping rhythm with the drums. It only lasted a few beats, but when they parted, it was long enough to fill some of the voids that had been empty inside her for far too long.

"I love you, Ty." It wasn't easy to say, but it wasn't as hard as she'd thought it would be either.

Ty grinned. "Told ya so." He spun her out fast, and a woman's laugh rose up around her. It was breezy and light, the kind of laugh she used to envy. And it was coming from her. From now on she hoped there'd be lots of laughs.

Ty had his head buried under the hood of the Piper, triple-checking it. Something hard poked his back and he jumped. His head smacked the hood and he spun around with a rag in his hands.

Dillon was standing there laughing, the crutch he'd just assailed Ty with innocently at his side. It matched the look on Dill's face. "I thought you were done. Stop being so nervous. Things'll go fine up there."

That was easy for him to say. "If you keep poking me with those things, I'm gonna take them from you."

"Go ahead. The doctor said I can give them up next week."

"Next week?" Ty tilted his head to the side and

gave him *the look*. Arms folded, legs hip-width apart, eyebrows lifted just a tiny bit.

But Dillon defended himself. "I'm not joking. I've been good for five weeks. No dancing and no climbing trees. It's time for these things to go."

Evie's voice called out from the hangar doors. "Ty, I rode Milkshake."

Her declaration sounded just as fishy as Dillon's. "You *rode* Milkshake? Since when do people ride cows?"

Emmitt came up behind her and shrugged. "She wanted to try. Milkshake's big enough."

What could Ty say to that? Emmitt loved Evie almost as much as he did. Only Ty was starting to think they were both spoiling her. He supposed a little bit of spoiling was okay.

"Is Mom here yet?"

"Not yet."

Evie craned her neck for a better look at the Piper's engine. Ty lifted her up so she could see. "When do I get to learn engine stuff?"

He heard a muffled chuckle and turned his head. Dillon was trying not to laugh. Ty guessed hearing a six-year-old ask that question was probably pretty funny. "How about we start on engine stuff after your birthday?"

"Like a birthday present?" She started squirming and Ty set her down before he dropped her.

Most kids wanted toys for their birthday. Evie

wanted to learn how a plane's engine worked. "Sure. But it's only part of your present."

Her eyes lit up. "What's the rest?"

Now that she'd started talking again, she had a question for everything. "You'll have to wait till next week to find out." He wanted to make sure Camille didn't change her mind about letting Evie take riding lessons.

A horn honked, and Camille waved to them from behind Buffy's window. At least the smoke coming out of her engine wasn't black today. Camille stepped out in jeans and a T-shirt. Ty started over. "There you are. Thought you'd be here sooner. Scared?"

She scoffed. "I sneaked out of my meeting five minutes early just so I could change out of my pencil skirt."

"Only five minutes?"

"Be thankful I managed that. The entire Raymond family was there today. A million pictures of wedding decorations and they're still not sure what they want."

"I thought they already picked everything."

"That was before."

"Before what?"

"Before Mrs. Raymond decided her daughter needed a proper runway to walk down and not one meant for small aircraft." She put her arms around him. "Don't worry, I got them to compromise. One month from now, your runway's going to be covered in lavender, rose petals and hay."

He grinned. "I'd expect nothing less from Nebraska's number one wedding planner."

"*Rising* wedding planner. None of the magazines have called me number one."

"Yet."

She gave Ty a kiss that might've lasted longer if Evie hadn't plowed into them, trying to wrap her arms around both of them at the same time.

Dillon put on a mock pouty face. "No hug and kiss for me?" Camille went over and slapped him playfully on the back of the head, then gave him a quick hug.

Emmitt was politely waiting for a chance to talk. "Evie asked if I could take her over to the nature center today."

There was the tiniest downturn of Camille's lips. "More bugs?"

Evie's eyes got big. "Just spiders. They've got a tarantula the size of a football."

To Camille's credit, she managed not to cringe. "You'll be with her the whole time?"

Emmitt nodded. "Avery too. She's around here somewhere with Nikki."

Camille gave the okay to take Evie out on the condition they had fun and left the bugs behind. Emmitt and Evie both assured her that would be no problem. They didn't leave right away though.

"Are you waiting to see me make a fool of myself?" Camille asked Evie, who flashed her a smile and a thumbs-up.

Camille started for the Piper, and Ty's heart started beating fast. Evie gave him a hug and whispered in his ear. "Don't be scared." It was the second time today someone had told him that. It didn't help.

Before Camille could get in, a cream-colored blur whizzed past her feet and started yipping circles around her. Camille kneeled down to pet Co-Coe, rubbing the dark brown tips of her ears just like she liked.

Avery and Nikki showed up five yips behind her. "I hear today's the big day," Avery said. Ty shot her a worried look. She'd promised not to say anything. "First time you get to handle take-off, huh?" He relaxed.

"That's right." Camille bit her bottom lip and looked at him. The tiniest flicker of doubt crossed her face. "Are you sure I'm ready for this?"

He was. "I have faith in you. And I'll be right there if anything happens."

She sucked in a breath, and Nikki started snapping pictures with her phone. The Piper's seats were front to back, not side to side. Ty got in the back and Camille climbed into the front. They got their headgear on and did a mic check.

"Ready?" he asked.

One big breath in and out. "Let's do this."

Ty looked out the window. Evie winked at him. "Whenever you're ready. Remember, I've got the same controllers you do, you're just the one in the pilot's seat today."

The key turned and the engine started. They moved down the runway. Ty peeked over her shoulder and double-checked their speed. "You're doing fine." She nodded and pulled back. The nose tipped but not quite enough, and they jumped a little to their left. Ty pulled back and evened things out.

"We're still good," he said. She was gonna have to pull back faster though or they were gonna lose the runway. He'd give her ten more seconds, then...

She did it.

Air swooped in under them as they left the ground. Camille let out a whoop and lifted her hands in victory. Ty grabbed the center stick and made sure they didn't nosedive while she did her victory cheer. When she took her control stick back, Ty let go of his.

"How high do you want to go?" she asked.

"You're the pilot. Your call."

They climbed to fifteen-hundred feet before she leveled things off. "You okay?" he asked.

"Amazing." She did a half turn and showed

him her smile to prove she meant it. Ty didn't need convincing; he could hear it in her voice.

Are you ready yet?

He told his inner voice to hold its horses and took a deep breath. "Do me a favor. Reach into that pouch hanging off your seat and pull out what's in there."

Camille dug her hand into the pouch and came out with a pen. She handed it to him. Ty groaned. "Not that. The square box." She dug back in and pulled out a navy blue velvet box. Her hand froze.

"Ty, what's this?" Her voice got quiet.

He leaned forward a little. "Do me another favor would you and open it up?"

With shaky fingers, Camille opened the lid on the box. A diamond engagement ring sat in the center. Nikki had given him very specific instructions on the right kind of ring to buy. The dos and don'ts of ring shopping.

In the end he'd ignored everything she'd said and gotten this vintage 1940s ring he'd found in an antiques shop. The woman who ran it had talked about clarity and old European settings and the white gold band. She'd pointed out imperfections and tried to upsell him with another ring, but Ty had known this ring belonged to Camille even with all its imperfections. It had been through a lot and come out all the more beautiful for it. It was meant for the spitfire in the pilot's seat.

"Oh, my." She turned to face him, and Ty took hold of the control stick again. He figured he'd better keep one hand on it for the next few minutes.

"Camille, I know it's fast, but when you find the thing you've been waiting your whole life for, it can't be fast enough. I love you, and I love Evie. And I know I ought to be down on one knee right now, but I was kinda hoping fifteen-hundred feet in the air was close enough." He took in a breath. "Will you marry me?"

For one minute, she didn't say anything. Didn't even blink. Then her eyes flooded and her head bobbed up and down. "Yes. Oh, yes." She craned her neck forward as far as she could and reached out one hand, trying to grab ahold of him. Ty grinned and gave her the kiss she wanted.

The plane tipped sideways, and they both pulled back. Ty leveled things off. "Mind if I do one quick thing before I give the power back to you?"

Suspicion crossed her eyes. "Okay…"

"Don't get scared. Remember, I was a Blue Angel."

"What does that mean?"

He double-checked his airspace. "Just trust me."

"With what?" He pulled back on the center stick. "Ty?"

The Piper spiraled upward, and Camille let out a scream. But it was an excited scream. If it had been anything else, he would've stopped. "It's a mini version of the vertical roll." One of Ty's old favorites. The Angels used to climb to fifteen-thousand feet. Ty topped them off at four thousand today.

It lasted two minutes, then he brought them back down to an even one-thousand feet. Camille was breathing hard, but she was smiling. "Are you gonna teach me to do that one day?"

He laughed. "When you're ready." Below them, Evie, Dillon, Nikki and the others all waved.

Camille looked at him. "Did they know you were proposing?"

"Evie got it out of me. That spiral was a little signal she and I worked out. It means you said yes."

She giggled and he gave her back control of the plane. "Where do you want to go?" she asked.

Ty leaned back in his seat. "From here? Anywhere we want."

Epilogue

Camille stepped up the ladder and peeked over Ty's shoulder at the engine. "The new Cessna's looking good."

He turned too fast and bopped his head on the hood. "One person on the ladder at a time." He shook his head and made tsking noises, but he didn't fool her for a second. His lopsided grin was in full swing today.

She got down and leaned against Cessna 1. It was sitting tandem to the new one. "Avery called. Smith got his leave. He'll be home in a few weeks and they're gonna have the wedding right away. They don't want to miss their chance again."

Ty wiped his hands on the rag. "It's about time. I bet Emmitt's happy. I thought he'd pout for a month when it got postponed."

"Evie too. She can't wait to be flower girl."

Ty moved the ladder back to the hangar. The Piper was tucked away today, resting. Camille gave it an affectionate pat. Ty came up behind her and wrapped his arms around her waist. He kissed that little spot just behind her ear that made her toes wiggle.

She turned and faced him. "You know, the first time we met, I thought you were pompous. Cute, but pompous."

He grinned. "And I thought you were pretty perfect. Then you started yelling at me and I knew it for sure." He went in for a kiss, and Camille tilted her head back to meet him. Even after all these months, every kiss felt just as special as the first.

Evie's voice called into the hangar. "Mom? Dad? Are you kissing *again*?" They turned to her, and Camille readied herself for the grossed-out face she knew was coming, but Evie was grinning. "Your two o'clock is here."

"Thanks, sweetie. By the way, have you seen your aunt Nikki?"

"Or your uncle Dillon?"

A mischievous grin spread across Evie's face. "They said if you asked to tell you they were fishing."

Fishing? Nikki should've known better. The only way she'd go near something scaly was if *fishing* was code for shopping at the mall. "And what are they really doing?"

There was Evie's icky face. "I think they're

having a picnic at her ranch. Uncle Dillon wrote her a poem. I heard him practicing it. He rhymed *sweet dreams* with *golden beams*." She giggled uncontrollably. Camille thought it was actually kinda cute.

Evie's icky face disappeared. "Is it okay if I go riding with Emmitt and Daisy? They said they'd show me that tree where the larks are nesting."

Ty looked at Camille. She shrugged. "Sure, honey," he said. "Have fun."

Outside the hangar, a group of six were hanging out, looking nervous. Ty and Camille introduced themselves. There were three men and three women, all in their thirties. It was a couples thing. *Fun.* Maybe she and Ty should start doing more couples things.

They already had Dillon and Nikki, that was a good start. Maybe they could find someone for Emmitt. Right now though, she wanted to make this day special for these couples in front of her. And that gave her an idea.

"We're a little bit nervous," said one woman with jet-black hair pulled into a ponytail. She was looking at her husband, who looked even more nervous than she did. His left nostril was flaring out in a strange way that didn't match the right.

"That's normal." Camille kept her voice soft and level just like Ty had taught her. It made a huge difference settling people's nerves.

"I suppose you two do this kind of thing all the time, don't you?" asked one man with thin lips and big muscles. He was trying to sound tough, but his eyes kept darting around, looking at the planes as if they might crash while sitting there on the ground.

She and Ty took them through some basics, then Camille laid her big idea on everyone. "Let's race. Twice around Sweet Dreams and back. Losers buy pie. They've got the best banana cream pie in the world right down the road from here."

A woman with bright blue eyes looked at Camille like she was speaking gibberish. "Race?"

"Yeah, girls against boys. It'll be fun."

"What's Sweet Dreams?" asked the big muscle guy.

"My sister's ranch." She pointed toward it and they all turned their heads. Everyone except Ty.

He gave her one of his looks. *You are in so much trouble.* "Camille…no."

"Scared?" She arched one eyebrow.

"Me? Never."

The woman with the dark ponytail perked up. "I'm game."

Not to be outdone, her husband chimed in with, "Me too." The *me too*s were seconded, and Camille shot Ty her smarty-pants smile. It was a new look she was working on.

He sighed. She leaned in close to him. "Tell you what. If you win, I'll let you replace Buffy."

His eyes widened. "You're serious?" She nodded, and he clapped his hands together. "All right. Guys, we've got a race to win."

The women all looked at her, suddenly nervous. "You're good, right? You can beat him?"

"Camille's a great pilot," Ty said.

"And how good are you?" asked one of the guys.

Camille smiled proudly at him. "Ty was a Blue Angel."

The three men laughed and started teasing their wives.

"I'll take my pie now."

"Hold the pie, eat our dust."

They separated guys from gals and got everyone buckled in. Then she and Ty met in the middle, toe to toe. He grinned at her. "May the better pilot win."

She grinned back. "Will do." He arched his eyebrow. It wasn't even close to what she could do. She gave him the double arch, then went in for a kiss. His lips warmed her up and she forgot all about their contest for a second. "I love you."

He pulled back. "I love you too. By the way, I told Evie she could get a pet tarantula for Christmas."

"What? Wait, are you—"

Ty darted for his plane. *He'd better be joking.* She wasn't about to let him throw her off like that though. She pushed pet tarantulas aside for now and ran for her plane. Ty made it first. The engine started up, and a minute later the men were gone.

The girls all groaned. "We already lost."

Camille checked her instruments and started down the runway. "We haven't lost anything yet. Hang on. This is a little trick I learned from a Blue Angel."

She brought the plane up and pushed the Cessna as fast as she could. They shot up high and spiraled forward, zipping ahead of Ty by a nose. She waved to him as she passed.

"Wow, you're really good," said the woman with the ponytail. The women were already crying victory, but Camille knew better. Never underestimate a Blue Angel.

* * * * *

Dear Reader,

I'm humbled and thrilled that you're joining me for my debut novel. When I was young, I used to love (or thought I did) heart-pounding adventures like riding roller coasters or walking a tightrope. My dream was to be a trapeze artist. Until one day I realized I was scared of heights.

We're all scared of something. Love, death, life…giant hairy spiders. The hero and heroine in my story are facing their own fears. And until they meet each other, they think they need to face them alone. As readers we all know better. It just takes Camille and Ty a little while to catch on.

Every summer, Chicago puts on an amazing air show over Lake Michigan featuring brave and skilled pilots from across the country, and sometimes the world. The Blue Angels often play a prominent role, along with others too numerous to list here. This is where the idea for my book sprang from, and I'm so glad it did.

I'm still learning to face my own fears. Luckily I've got an amazing husband and a fluff-ball of a cat to encourage me. Soon I plan to tackle my first flying lesson. Maybe not the wisest idea for someone scared of heights, but the adventurer in me still longs to walk those tightropes. So I'm facing my fears head-on. And whether it's your husband, cat or God helping you along, I hope you find a way to face yours too.

Warmest Wishes,
Christine Raymond

Get 4 FREE REWARDS!

We'll send you 2 FREE Books plus 2 FREE Mystery Gifts.

Harlequin Heartwarming Larger-Print books will connect you to uplifting stories where the bonds of friendship, family and community unite.

FREE
Value Over
$20

HARLEQUIN SELECTS COLLECTION

19 FREE BOOKS IN ALL!

From Robyn Carr to RaeAnne Thayne to Linda Lael Miller and Sherryl Woods we promise (actually, GUARANTEE!) each author in the Harlequin Selects collection has seen their name on the *New York Times* or *USA TODAY* bestseller lists!